A Bride from the Bush

A Bride from
the Bush

E.W. Hornung

MINT EDITIONS

A Bride from the Bush was first published in 1890.

This edition published by Mint Editions 2021.

ISBN 9781513280622 | E-ISBN 9781513285641

Published by Mint Editions®

MINT
EDITIONS

minteditionbooks.com

Publishing Director: Jennifer Newens
Design & Production: Rachel Lopez Metzger
Project Manager: Micaela Clark
Typesetting: Westchester Publishing Services

Contents

I

A Letter from Alfred

There was consternation in the domestic camp of Mr. Justice Bligh on the banks of the Thames. It was a Sunday morning in early summer. Three-fourths of the family sat in ominous silence before the mockery of a well-spread breakfast-table: Sir James and Lady Bligh and their second son, Granville. The eldest son—the missing complement of this family of four—was abroad. For many months back, and, in fact, down to this very minute, it had been pretty confidently believed that the young man was somewhere in the wilds of Australia; no one had quite known where, for the young man, like most vagabond young men, was a terribly meagre corespondent; nor had it ever been clear why any one with leisure and money, and of no very romantic turn, should have left the beaten track of globe-trotters, penetrated to the wilderness, and stayed there—as Alfred Bligh had done. Now, however, all was plain. A letter from Brindisi, just received, explained everything; Alfred's movements, so long obscure, were at last revealed, and in a lurid light—that, as it were, of the bombshell that had fallen and burst upon the Judge's breakfast-table. For Alfred was on his way to England with an Australian wife; and this letter from Brindisi, was the first that his people had heard of it, or of her.

"Of course," said Lady Bligh, in her calm and thoughtful manner, "it was bound to happen sooner or later. It might have happened very much sooner; and, indeed, I often wished that it would; for Alfred must be—what? Thirty?"

"Quite," said Granville; "I am nearly that myself."

"Well, then," said Lady Bligh gently, looking tenderly at the Judge (whose grave eyes rested upon the sunlit lawn outside), "from one point of view—a selfish one—we ought to consider ourselves the most fortunate of parents. And this news should be a matter for rejoicing, as it would be, if—if it were only less sudden, and wild, and—and—"

Her voice trembled; she could not go on.

"And alarming," added Granville briskly, pulling himself together and taking an egg.

Then the Judge spoke.

"I should like," he said, "to hear the letter read slowly from beginning to end. Between us, we have not yet given it a fair chance; we have got only the drift of it; we may have overlooked something. Granville, perhaps you will read the letter aloud to your mother and me?"

Granville, who had just laid open his egg with great skill, experienced a moment's natural annoyance at the interruption. To stop to read a long letter now was, he felt, treating a good appetite shabbily, to say nothing of the egg. But this was not a powerful feeling; he concealed it. He had a far stronger appetite than the mere relish for food; the intellectual one. Granville had one of the nicest intellects at the Junior Bar. His intellectual appetite was so hearty, and even voracious, that it could be gratified at all times and places, and not only by the loaves and fishes of full-bodied wit, but by the crumbs and fishbones of legal humour—such as the reading aloud of indifferent English and ridiculous sentiments in tones suitable to the most chaste and classic prose. This he had done in court with infinite gusto, and he did it now as he would have done it in court.

"'My dear Mother'" (he began reading, through a single eyeglass that became him rather well),—"'Before you open this letter you'll see that I'm on my way home! I am sorry I haven't written you for so long, and *very* sorry I didn't before I sailed. I should think when I last wrote was from Bindarra. But I must come at once to my great news—which Heaven knows how I'm to tell you, and how you'll take it when I do. Well, I will, in two words—the fact is, *I'm married*! My wife is the daughter of "the boss of Bindarra"—in other words, a "squatter" with a "run" (or territory) as big as a good many English counties.'"

The crisp forensic tones were dropped for an explanatory aside. "He evidently *means*—father" (Granville nearly said "my lord," through force of habit), "that his father-in-law is the squatter; not his wife, which is what he *says*. He writes in such a slipshod style. I should also think he means that the territory in question is equal in size to certain English counties, individually (though this I venture to doubt), and not—what you would infer—to several counties put together. His literary manner was always detestable, poor old chap; and, of course, Australia was hardly likely to improve it."

The interpolation was not exactly ill-natured; but it was received in silence; and Granville's tones, as he resumed the reading, were even more studiously unsympathetic than before.

"'Of my Bride I will say very little; for you will see her in a week at most. As for myself, I can only tell you, dear Mother, that I am the very luckiest and happiest man on earth!" ("A brave statement," Granville murmured in parenthesis; "but they all make it.") "'She is typically Australian, having indeed been born and bred in the Bush, and is the first to admit it, being properly proud of her native land; but, if you knew the Australians as I do, this would not frighten you. Far from it, for the typical Australian is one of the very highest if not *the* highest development of our species.'" (Granville read that sentence with impressive gravity, and with such deference to the next as to suggest no kind of punctuation, since the writer had neglected it.) "'But as you, my dear Mother, are the very last person in the world to be prejudiced by mere mannerisms, I won't deny that she has one or two—*though, mind you, I like them!* And, at least, you may look forward to seeing the most beautiful woman you ever saw in your life—though I say it.

"'Feeling sure that you will, as usual, be "summering" at Twickenham, I make equally sure that you will be able and willing to find room for us; at the same time, we will at once commence looking out for a little place of our own in the country, with regard to which we have plans which will keep till we see you. But, while we are with you, I thought I would be able to show my dear girl the principal sights of the Old Country, which, of course, are mostly in or near town, and which she is dying to see.

> Dear Mother,
>
> I know I *ought* to have consulted you, or at least told you, beforehand. The whole thing was impulsive, I admit. But if you and my Father will forgive me for this—take my word for it, you will soon find out that it is all you have to forgive! Of course, I am writing to my Father as much as to you in this letter—as he will be the first to understand. With dearest love to you both (not forgetting Gran), in which Gladys joins me (though she doesn't know I am saying so).
>
> Believe me as ever,
>
> Your affectionate Son,
> Alfred

"Thank you," said the Judge, shortly.

The soft dark eyes of Lady Bligh were wet with tears.

"I think," she said, gently, "it is a very tender letter. I know of no man but Alfred that could write such a boyish, simple letter—not that

I don't enjoy your clever ones, Gran. But then Alfred never yet wrote to me without writing himself down the dear, true-hearted, affectionate fellow he is; only here, of course, it comes out doubly. But does he not mention her maiden name?"

"No, he doesn't," said Granville. "You remarked the Christian name, though? Gladys! I must say it sounds unpromising. Mary, Eliza, Maria—one would have rather liked a plain, homely, farm-yard sort of name for a squatter's daughter. But Ermyntrude, or Elaine, or Gladys! These are names of ill-omen; you expect de Vere coming after them, or even worse."

"What *is* a squatter, Gran?" asked Lady Bligh abruptly.

"A squatter? I don't know," said Gran, paring the ham daintily as he answered. "I don't know, I'm sure; something to do with bushranging, I should imagine—but I really can't tell you."

But there was a set of common subjects of which Gran was profoundly and intentionally ignorant; and it happened that Greater Britain was one of them. If he had known for certain whether Sydney (for instance) was a town or a colony or an island, he would have kept the knowledge carefully to himself, and been thoroughly ashamed of it. And it was the same with other subjects understood of the Board-scholars. This queer temper of mind is not indeed worth analysing; nevertheless, it is peculiar to a certain sort of clever young fellows, and Granville Bligh was a very fair specimen of the clever young fellow. He was getting on excellently at the Bar, for so young a man. He also wrote a little, with plenty of impudence and epigram, if nothing else. But this was not his real line. Still, what he did at all, he did more or less cleverly. There was cleverness in every line of his smooth dark face; there was uncommon shrewdness in his clear gray eyes. His father had the same face and the same eyes—with this difference added to the differences naturally due to age: there were wisdom, and dignity, and humanity in the face and glance of the Judge; but the nobility of expression thus given was not inherited by the Judge's younger son.

The Judge spoke again, breaking a silence of some minutes:—

"As you say, Mildred, it seems to have been all very wild and sudden; but when we have said this, we have probably said the worst there is to say. At least, let us hope so. Of my own knowledge many men have gone to Australia, as Alfred went, and come back with the best of wives. I seem to have heard, Granville, that that is what Merivale did; and I have met few more admirable women than Mrs. Merivale."

"It certainly is the case, sir," said Granville, who had been patronised to some extent by Merivale, Q.C. "But Mrs. Merivale was scarcely 'born and bred in the Bush'; and if she had what poor Alfred, perhaps euphemistically, calls 'mannerisms'—I have detected no traces of any myself—when Merivale married her, at least she had money."

"Your sister-in-law may have 'money,' too," said Sir James, with somewhat scornful emphasis. "That is of no consequence at all. Your brother has enough for both, and more than enough for a bachelor."

There was no need to remind the young man of that; it had been a sore point, and even a raw one, with Granville since his boyhood; for it was when the brothers were at school together—the younger in the Sixth Form, the elder in the Lower Fifth—and it was already plain which one would benefit the most by "private means," that a relative of Sir James had died, leaving all her money to Alfred.

Granville coloured slightly—very slightly—but observed:—

"It is a good thing he has."

"What do you mean?" the Judge asked, with some asperity.

"That he needs it," said Granville, significantly.

Sir James let the matter drop, and presently, getting up, went out by the open French window, and on to the lawn. It was not his habit to snub his son; he left that to the other judges, in court. But Lady Bligh remonstrated in her own quiet way—a way that had some effect even upon Granville.

"To sneer at your brother's inferior wits, my son, is not in quite nice taste," she said; "and I may tell you, now, that I did not at all care for your comments upon his letter."

Granville leant back in his chair and laughed pleasantly.

"How seriously you take one this morning! But it is small wonder that you should, for the occasion is a sufficiently serious one, in all conscience; and indeed, dear mother, I am as much put out as you are. Nay," Granville added, smiling blandly, "don't say that you're *not* put out, for I can see that you *are*. And we have reason to be put out"—he became righteously indignant—"all of us. I wouldn't have thought it of Alfred, I wouldn't indeed! No matter whom he wanted to marry, he ought at least to have written first, instead of being in such a violent hurry to bring her over. It is treating *you*, dear mother, to say the best of it, badly; and as for the Judge, it is plain that he is quite upset by the unfortunate affair."

"We have no right to assume that it is unfortunate, Gran."

"Well, I hope it is not, that's *all*," said Gran, with great emphasis. "I hope it is not, for poor Alfred's sake. Yet, as you know, mother, he's the very kind of old chap to get taken in and imposed upon; and—I tell you frankly—I tremble for him. If he is the victim of a designing woman, I am sorry for him, from my soul I am! If he has married in haste—and he has—to repent at leisure—as he may—though this is trite and detestable language, I pity him, from my soul I do! You have already rebuked me—I don't say unjustly—for making what, I admit, had the appearance of an odious and egotistical comparison; I will guard against conveying a second impression of that kind; yet I think I may safely say, without bragging, that I know the world rather better than old Alfred does. Well, I have, I will not say my fears, but my dreads; and I cannot help having them. If they are realised, no one will sympathise with poor dear Alfred more deeply than I shall."

Lady Bligh looked keenly at her eloquent son; a half-smile played about her lips: she understood him, to some extent.

"But what if your fears are *not* realised?" she said, quietly.

"Why, then," said Gran, less fluently, "then I—oh, of course, I shall be delighted beyond words; no one will be more delighted than I."

"Then you shall see," said Lady Bligh, rising, with a sweet and hopeful smile, "that is how it is going to turn out; I have a presentiment that it will all turn out for the best. So there is only one thing to be done—we must prepare to welcome her to our hearts!"

Granville shrugged his shoulders, but his mother did not see him; she had gone quietly from the room and was already climbing (slowly, for she was stout) the stairs that led up to her own snuggery on the first floor. This little room was less of a boudoir than a study, and more like an office than either, for it was really a rather bare little room. Its most substantial piece of furniture was a large unlovely office-table, and its one picture was framed in the window-sashes—a changeful picture of sky and trees, and lawn and river, painted this morning in the most radiant tints of early summer. At the office-table, which was littered with letters and pamphlets, Lady Bligh spent diligent hours every day. She was a person of both mental and manual activity, with public sympathies and interests that entailed an immense correspondence. She was, indeed, one of the most charitable and benevolent of women, and was to some extent a public woman. But we have nothing to do with her public life, and, on this Sunday morning, no more had she.

There were no pictures on the walls, but there were photographs upon the chimney-piece. Lady Bligh stood looking at them for an unusually long time—in fact, until the sound of the old church bells, coming in through the open window, called her away.

One of the photographs was of the Judge—an excellent one, in which the dear old gentleman looked his very best, dignified but kindly. Another was a far too flattering portrait of Granville. A third portrait was that of an honest, well-meaning, and rather handsome face, with calm dark eyes, exactly like Lady Bligh's; and this was the erratic Alfred. But the photograph that Lady Bligh looked at longest, and most fondly, was a faded one of Alfred and Granville as mere schoolboys. She loved her two sons so dearly! One of them was much changed, and becoming somewhat spoilt, to phrase it mildly; yet that son was rather clever, and his mother saw his talents through a strong binocular, and his faults with her eyes at the wrong end of it; and she loved him in spite of the change in him, and listened—at least with tolerance—to the airings of a wit that was always less good natured, and generally less keen, than she imagined it. But the other son had never changed at all; even his present fatal letter showed that. He was still a boy at heart—a wild, stupid, affectionate schoolboy. There was no denying it: in his mother's heart the elder son was the best beloved of the two.

And it was this one who had married with so much haste and mystery—the favourite son, the son with money, the son who might have married any one he pleased. It was hard to choke down prejudice when this son was bringing home a wife from the Bush, of all places!

What would she be like? What *could* she be like?

II

HOME IN STYLE

H e must be mad!" said Granville, flourishing a telegram in his hand. "He must be very fond of her," Lady Bligh replied, simply.

Granville held the telegram at arm's length, and slowly focussed it with his eyeglass. He had already declaimed it twice, once with horror in his voice, once with a running accompaniment of agreeable raillery. His third reading was purely compassionate, in accordance with his latest theory regarding the mental condition of the sender.

"'Arrived both well. Chartered launch take us Gravesend Twickenham; show her river. Join us if possible Westminster Bridge 3 o'clock.—Alfred.'"

Granville sighed.

"Do you comprehend it, dear mother? I think I do, at last, though the prepositions *are* left to the imagination. He has saved at least twopence over those prepositions—which, of course, is an item, even in a ten-pound job."

"You don't mean to say it will cost him ten pounds?"

"Every penny of it: it would cost you or me, or any ordinary person, at least a fiver. I am allowing for Alfred's being let in rather further than any one else would be."

"At all events," said Lady Bligh, "you will do what he asks you; you will be at Westminster at the time he mentions?"

Granville shrugged his shoulders. "Certainly, if you wish it."

"I think it would be kind."

"Then I will go, by all means."

"Thank you—and Granville! I do wish you would give up sneering at your brother's peculiarities. He *does* do odd and impulsive things, we know; and there is no denying the extravagance of steaming up the river all the way from Gravesend. But, after all, he has money, and no doubt he wants to show his wife the Thames, and to bring her home in a pleasant fashion, full of pleasant impressions; and upon my word," said Lady Bligh, "I never heard of a prettier plan in my life! So go, my dear boy, and meet them, and make them happier still. If that is possible, no one could do it more gracefully than you, Gran!"

Granville acknowledged the compliment, and promised; and punctually at three he was at Westminster Bridge, watching with considerable interest the rapid approach of a large launch—a ridiculously large one for the small number of people on board. She had, in fact, only two passengers, though there was room for fifty. One of the two was Alfred, whose lanky figure was unmistakable at any distance; and the dark, straight, strapping young woman at his side was, of course, Alfred's wife.

The meeting between the brothers was hearty enough, but it might have been more entirely cordial had there been a little less effusiveness on one side—not Granville's. But Alfred—who was dressed in rough tweed clothes of indeterminate cut, and had disfigured himself with a beard—was so demonstrative in his greeting that the younger brother could not help glancing anxiously round to assure himself that there was no one about who knew him. It was a relief to him to be released and introduced to the Bride.

"Gladys, this is Gran come to meet us—as I knew he would—like the brick he is, and always was!"

Gran was conscious of being scrutinised keenly by the finest dark eyes he had ever encountered in his life; but the next moment he was shaking his sister-in-law's hand, and felt that it was a large hand—a trifling discovery that filled Granville with a subtile sense of satisfaction. But the Bride was yet to open her lips.

"How do you do?" she said, the olive tint of her cheek deepening slightly. "It was awfully nice of you to come; I *am* glad to see you—I have heard such lots about you, you know!"

It was said so glibly that the little speech was not, perhaps, exactly extempore: and it was spoken—every word of it—with a twang that, to sensitive ears like Granville's, was simply lacerating. Granville winced, and involuntarily dropped his eyeglass; but otherwise he kept a courteous countenance, and made a sufficiently civil reply.

As for Alfred, he, of course, noticed nothing unusual in his wife's accents; he was used to them; and, indeed, it seemed to Granville that Alfred spoke with a regrettable drawl himself.

"You've got to play showman, Gran," said he, when some natural questions had been hurriedly put and tersely answered (by which time they were opposite Lambeth Palace). "I've been trying, but I'm a poor hand at it; indeed, I'm a poor Londoner, and always was: below Blackfriars I was quite at sea, and from here to Richmond I'm as ignorant as a brush."

"No; he's no good at all," chimed in the Bride, pleasantly.

"Well, I'm not well up in it, either," said Gran, warily.

This was untrue, however. Granville knew his Thames better than most men—it was one of the things he *did* know. But he had a scholar's reverence for classic ground; and in a young man who revered so very little, this was remarkable, if it was not affectation. Granville would have suffered tortures rather than gravely point out historic spots to a person whose ideas of history probably went no farther back than the old Colonial digging days; he would have poured sovereigns into the sea as readily as the coin of sacred associations into Gothic ears. At least, so he afterwards said, when defending his objection to interpreting the Thames for his sister-in-law's benefit.

"What nonsense!" cried Alfred, good-humouredly. "You know all about it—at all events, you used to. There—we've gone and let her miss Lambeth Palace! Look, dear, quick, while it's still in sight—that's where the Archbishop of Canterbury hangs out."

"Oh," said Gladys, "I've heard of *him*."

"And isn't that Cheyne Walk, or some such place, that we're coming to on the right there?" said Alfred.

"Yes," said Granville, briefly; "that's Cheyne Walk."

Luckily the Bride asked no questions—indeed, she was inclined to be silent—for of all localities impossible to discuss with an uneducated person, Granville felt that Chelsea and Cheyne Walk were the most completely out of the question. And that the Bride was a sadly uneducated person was sufficiently clear, if only from her manner of speaking. Granville accepted the fact with creditable equanimity—he had prophesied as much—and sat down to smoke a cigarette and to diagnose, if he could, this new and wonderful dialect of his sister-in-law. It was neither Cockney nor Yankee, but a nasal blend of both: it was a lingo that declined to let the vowels run alone, but trotted them out in ill-matched couples, with discordant and awful consequences; in a word, it was Australasiatic of the worst description. Nor was the speech of Alfred free from the taint—Alfred, whose pronunciation at least had been correct before he went out; while the common colloquialisms of the pair made Granville shudder.

"If I did not hope for such surprisingly good looks," said he to himself, "yet even *I* was not prepared for *quite* so much vulgarity! Poor dear Alfred!"

And Granville sighed, complacently.

Yet, as she leant upon the rail in the summer sunlight, silent and pensive, there was certainly no suggestion of vulgarity in her attitude; it was rather one of unstudied grace and ease. Nor was there anything at all vulgar in the quiet travelling dress that fitted her tall full form so closely and so well. Nor was her black hair cut down to within an inch of her eyebrows—as, of course, it should have been—or worn in a fringe at all. Nor was there anything the least objectionable in the poise of the small graceful head, or in the glance of the bold dark eyes, or in the set of the full, firm, crimson lips; and thus three more excellent openings—for the display of vulgarity—were completely thrown away. In fact, if she had never spoken, Granville would have been at a loss to find a single fault in her. Alas! about her speech there could be no two opinions—it bewrayed her.

Presently Alfred sat down beside his brother, and began to tell him everything, and did all the talking; while the Bride still stood watching the shifting panorama of the banks, and the golden sunlight upon the water, and the marvellous green of all green things. It was practically her first experience of this colour. And still she asked no questions, her interest being perhaps too intense; and so the showman-business was forgotten, to the great relief of Granville; and the time slipped quickly by. At last—and quite suddenly—the Bride clapped her hands, and turned with sparkling eyes to her husband: they had entered that splendid reach below Richmond, and the bridges were in sight, with the hill beyond.

"I give this best!" she cried. "It *does* knock spots out of the Yarra and the Murray after all!"

Alfred glanced uneasily at his brother, but found an impassive face.

"Come, old fellow," said Alfred, "do your duty; jump up and tell her about these places."

So at last Granville made an effort to do so; he got up and went to the side of the Bride; and presently he was exercising a discreet if not a delicate vein of irony, that was peculiarly his own.

"That was Kew we passed just now—you must see the gardens there," he said; "and this is Richmond."

"Kew and Richmond!" exclaimed the Bride, innocently. "How rum! We have a Kew and a Richmond in Melbourne."

"Ah!" said Gran. "I don't fancy the theft was on our side. But look at this gray old bridge—picturesque, isn't it?—and I dare say you have nothing like it out there. And there, you see—up on the left yonder—is Richmond Hill. Rather celebrated, Richmond Hill: you may have heard of it; there was a lass that lived there once."

"Yes—what of her?"

"Oh, she was neat and had sweet eyes—or sweet, with neat eyes—I really forget which. And there was a somebody or other who said he'd resign any amount of crowns—the number wasn't specified—to call her his. He was pretty safe in saying that—unless, indeed, he meant crown-*pieces*—which, now I think of it, would be rather an original reading."

"Alfred," said the Bride abruptly, "are we nearly there?"

"Not far off," said Alfred.

Granville bit his lip. "We are very nearly there," he said; "this is the beginning of Twickenham."

"Then where's the Ferry?" said the Bride. "I know all about 'Twickenham Ferry'; we once had a storekeeper—a new chum—who used to sing about it like mad. Show it me."

"There, then: it crosses by the foot of the island: it's about to cross now. Now, in a minute, I'll show you Pope's old place; we don't go quite so far—in fact, here we are—but you'll be able just to see it, I think."

"The Pope!" said Gladys. "I never knew *he* lived in England!"

"No more he does. Not *the* Pope—*Pope*; a man of the name of Pope: a scribbler: a writing-man: in fact, a poet."

The three were leaning over the rail, shoulder to shoulder, and watching eagerly for the first glimpse of the Judge's retreat through the intervening trees. Granville was in the middle. The Bride glanced at him sharply, and opened her lips to say something which—judging by the sudden gleam of her dark eyes—might possibly have been rather too plain-spoken. But she never said it; she merely left Granville's side, and went round to the far side of her husband, and slipped her hand through his arm. Granville walked away.

"Are we there?" whispered Gladys.

"Just, my darling. Look, that's the house—the one with the tall trees and the narrow lawn."

"Hoo-jolly-ray!"

"Hush, Gladdie! For Heaven's sake don't say anything like that before my mother! There she is on the lawn, waving her handkerchief. We'll wave ours back to her. The dear mother! Whatever you do, darling girl, don't say anything of that sort to *her*. It would be Greek to my mother and the Judge, and they mightn't like it."

III

PINS AND NEEDLES

S lanting mellow sunbeams fell pleasantly upon the animated face of the Bride, as she stepped lightly across the gangway from the steam-launch to the lawn; and, for one moment, her tall supple figure stood out strikingly against the silver river and the pale eastern sky. In that moment a sudden dimness came over Lady Bligh's soft eyes, and with outstretched arms she hurried forward to press her daughter to her heart. It was a natural motherly impulse, but, even if Lady Bligh had stopped to think, she would have made sure of being met half-way. She was not, however, and the mortification of the moment was none the less intense because it was invisible. The Bride refused to be embraced. She was so tall that it would have been impossible for Lady Bligh to kiss her against her will, but it never came to that; the unbending carriage and man-like outstretched hand spoke plainly and at once—and were understood. But Lady Bligh coloured somewhat, and it was an unfortunate beginning, for every one noticed it; and the Judge, who was hurrying towards them across the lawn at the time, there and then added a hundred per cent of ceremony to his own greeting, and received his daughter-in-law as he would have received any other stranger.

"I am very happy to see you," he said, when Alfred had introduced them—the Judge waited for that. "Welcome, indeed; and I hope you have received agreeable impressions of our River Thames."

"Oh, rather!" said Gladys, smiling unabashed upon the old gentleman. "We've no rivers like it in Australia. I've just been saying so."

Granville, who had been watching for a change in his mother's expression when she should first hear the Bride speak, was not disappointed. Lady Bligh winced perceptibly. Judges, however, may be relied upon to keep their countenances, if anybody may; it is their business; Sir James was noted for it, and he merely said dryly, "I suppose not," and that was all.

And then they all walked up the lawn together to where tea awaited them in the veranda. The Bride's dark eyes grew round at sight of the gleaming silver teapot and dainty Dresden china; she took her seat in silence in a low wicker chair, while the others talked around her; but presently she was heard exclaiming:—

"No, thanks, no milk, and I'll sweeten it myself, please."

"But it's cream," said Lady Bligh, good-naturedly, pausing with the cream-jug in the air.

"The same thing," returned Gladys. "We never took any on the station, so I like it better without; and it can't be too strong, if you please. We didn't take milk," she turned to explain to Sir James, "because, in a general way, our only cow was a tin one, and we preferred no milk at all. We ran sheep, you see, not cattle."

"A tin cow!" said Sir James.

"She means they only had condensed milk," said Alfred, roaring with laughter.

"But our cow is *not* tin," said Lady Bligh, smiling, as she still poised the cream-jug; "will you not change your mind?"

"No, thanks," said the Bride stoutly.

It was another rather awkward moment, for it did seem as though Gladys was disagreeably independent. And Alfred, of all people, made the moment more awkward still, and, indeed, more uncomfortable than any that had preceded it.

"Gladdie," he exclaimed in his airiest manner, "you're a savage! A regular savage, as I've told you over and over again!"

No one said anything. Gladys smiled, and Alfred chuckled over his pleasantry. But it was a pleasantry that contained a most unpleasant truth. The others felt this, and it made them silent. It was a relief to all—with the possible exception of the happy pair, neither of whom appeared to be over-burdened with self-consciousness—when Lady Bligh carried off Gladys, and delivered her in her own room into the safe keeping of Miss Bunn, her appointed maid.

This girl, Bunn, presently appeared in the servants' hall, sat down in an interesting way, and began to twirl her thumbs with great ostentation. Being questioned, in fulfilment of her artless design, she said that she was not wanted upstairs. Being further questioned, she rattled off a string of the funny things Mrs. "*H*alfred" had said to her along with a feeble imitation of Mrs. "*H*alfred's" very funny way of saying them. This is not a matter of importance; but it was the making of Bunn below stairs; so long as Mrs. Alfred remained in the house, her maid's popularity as a kitchen entertainer was assured.

The Bride wished to be alone; at all events she desired no personal attendance. What should she want with a maid? A lady's-maid was a "fixing" she did not understand, and did not wish to understand; she had said so plainly, and that she didn't see where Miss Bunn "came in"; and then Miss Bunn had gone out, in convulsions. And now the Bride was alone at last, and stood pensively gazing out of her open window at the wonderful green trees and the glittering river, at the deep cool shadows and the pale evening sky; and delight was in her bold black eyes; yet a certain sense of something not quite as it ought to be—a sensation at present vague and undefined—made her graver than common. And so she stood until the door was burst suddenly open, and a long arm curled swiftly round her waist, and Alfred kissed her.

"My darling! tell me quickly—"

"Stop!" said Gladys. "I'll bet I guess what it is you want me to tell you! Shall I?"

"Yes, if you can, for I certainly do want you to tell me something."

"Then it's what I think of your people!"

"How you like them," Alfred amended. "Yes, that was it. Well, then?"

"Well, then—I like your mother. She has eyes like yours, Alfred, large and still and kind, and she is big and motherly."

"Then, oh, my darling, why on earth didn't you kiss her?"

"Kiss her? Not *me*! Why should I?"

"She meant to kiss you; I saw she did."

"Don't you believe it! Even if she had, it would have been only for your sake. You wait a little bit; wait till she knows me, and if she wants to kiss me then—let her!"

Alfred was pained by his young wife's tone; he had never before heard her speak so strangely, and her eyes were wistful. He did not quite understand her, but he did not try to, then; he varied the subject.

"How about Gran?"

"Oh, that Gran!" cried Gladys. "I can't suffer him at all."

"Can't suffer Gran! What on earth do you mean, Gladys?"

"I mean that he was just a little beast in the boat! You think he was as glad to see you as you were him, because you judge by yourself; but not a bit of it; I know better. It was all put on with him, and a small 'all' too. Then you asked him to tell me about the places we passed, and he only laughed at me. Ah, you may laugh at people without moving a muscle, but people may see it all the same; and I did, all along; and just before we got here I very near told him so. If I had, I'd have given him one, you stake your life!"

"I'm glad you didn't," said Alfred devoutly, but in great trouble. "*I* never heard him say anything to rankle like that; I thought he was very jolly, if you ask me. And really, Gladdie, old Gran's as good a fellow as ever lived; besides which, he has all the brains of the family."

"Perhaps," said Gladys, softening, "my old man has got a double share of something better than brains!"

"Nonsense, darling! But at least the Judge was pleasant; what did you think of the Judge?"

"I funked him."

"Good gracious! Why?"

"He's so dreadfully dignified; and he looks you through and through—not nastily, like Gran does, but as if you were something funny in a glass case."

"What stuff and nonsense, Gladdie! You're making me miserable. Look here: talk to the Judge: draw him out a bit. That's all he wants, and he likes it."

"What am I to call him—'Judge'?"

"No: not that: never that. For the present, 'Sir James,' I think."

"And what am I to talk about?"

"Oh, anything—Australia. Interest him about the Bush. Try, dearest, at dinner—to please me."

"Very well," said Gladys; "I'll have a shot."

And she had one, though it was not quite the kind of shot Alfred would have recommended—at any rate, not for a first shot. For, on thinking it over, it seemed to Gladys that, with relation to the Bush, nothing could interest a Judge so much as the manner of administering the law there, which she knew something about. Nor was the subject unpromising or unsafe: it was only her way of leading up to it that was open to criticism.

"I suppose, Sir James," she began, "you have lots of trying to do?"

"Trying?" said the Judge, looking up from his soup; for the Bride had determined not to be behindhand in keeping her promise, and had opened the attack thus early.

"As if he were a tailor!" thought Granville. "Trials, sir," he suggested suavely. He was sitting next Gladys, who was on the Judge's right.

"Ah, trials!" said the Judge with a faint—a very faint—smile. "Oh, yes—a great number."

A sudden thought struck Gladys. She became the interested instead of the interesting party. She forgot the Bush, and stared at her father-in-law in sudden awe.

"Are there many murder trials among them, Sir James?"

By the deliberate manner with which he went on with his soup, the Judge apparently did not hear the question. But Lady Bligh and Alfred heard it, and were horrified; while Granville looked grave, and listened for more with all his ears. He had not to wait long. Gladys feared she had expressed herself badly, and quickly tried again.

"What I mean is—Sir James—do you often have to go and put on the black cap, and sentence poor unfortunate people to be hung? Because that can't be very nice, Sir James—is it?"

A faint flush mounted into the Judge's pale cheeks. "It is not of frequent occurrence," he said stiffly.

Granville, sitting next her, might easily have stopped his sister-in-law by a word or a sign before this; but Alfred was practically hidden from her by the lamp, and though he tried very hard to kick her under the table, he only succeeded in kicking footstools and table-legs; and Lady Bligh was speechless.

The Bride, however, merely thought that Alfred had exaggerated the ease with which his father was to be drawn out. But she had not given in yet. That would have been contrary to her nature.

"What a good thing!" she said. "It would be so—so horrid, if it happened *very* often, to wake up and say to yourself, 'That poor fellow's got to swing in a minute or two; and it's me that's done it!' It would be a terror if that was to happen every week or so; and I'm glad for your sake, Sir James—"

She broke off suddenly; why, it is difficult to say, for no one had spoken; but perhaps that was the very reason. At all events, she remembered her experience of Bush law, and got to her point, now, quickly enough.

"I was once at a trial myself, Sir James, in the Bush," she said (and there was certainly a general sense of relief). "My own father was boss—or Judge, if you like—that trip. There were only four people there; the sergeant, who was jailer and witness as well, father, the prisoner, and me; I looked on."

"Is your father a member of the Colonial Bar?" inquired Sir James, mildly.

"Lord, no, Sir James! He's only a magistrate. Why, he'd only got to remand the poor chap down to Cootamundra; yet he had to consult gracious knows how many law-books (the sergeant had them ready) to do it properly!"

They all laughed; but there was a good deal that ought not to have been laughed at. A moment before, when her subject was about as unfortunate as it could have been, she had chosen her mere words with a certain amount of care and good taste; but now that she was on her native heath, and blameless in matter, her manner had become dreadful—her expressions were shocking—her twang worse than ever. The one subject that she was at home in excited her to an unseemly degree. No sooner, then, had the laugh subsided than Lady Bligh seized upon the conversation, hurled it well over the head of the Bride, and kept it there, high and dry, until the end of dessert; then she sailed away to the drawing-room with the unconscious offender.

It was time to end this unconsciousness.

"My dear," said Lady Bligh, "will you let me give you a little lecture?"

"Certainly," said Gladys, opening her eyes rather wide, but won at once by the old lady's manner.

"Then, my dear, you should never interrogate people about their professional duties, least of all a judge. Sir James does not like it; and even I never dream of doing it."

"Goodness gracious!" cried the Bride. "Have I been and put my foot in it, then?"

"You have said nothing that really matters," Lady Bligh replied hastily; and she determined to keep till another time some observations that were upon her mind on the heads of "slang" and "twang;" for the poor girl was blushing deeply, and seemed, at last, thoroughly uncomfortable; which was not what Lady Bligh wanted at all.

"Only, I must tell you," Lady Bligh continued, "it *was* an unfortunate choice to hit upon the death-sentence for a subject of conversation. All judges are sensitive about it; Sir James is particularly so. But there! there is nothing for you to look grieved about, my dear. No one will think anything more of such a trifle; and, of course, out in Australia everything must be quite different."

Gladys bridled up at once; she would have no allowances made for herself at the expense of her country. It is a point on which Australians are uncommonly sensitive, small blame to them.

"Don't you believe it!" she cried vigorously. "You mustn't go blaming Australia, Lady Bligh; it's no fault of Australia's. It's *my* fault—*my* ignorance—*me* that's to blame! Oh, please to remember: whenever I do or say anything wrong, you've not to excuse me because I'm an

Australian! Australia's got nothing to do with it; it's me that doesn't know what's what, and has got to learn!"

Her splendid eyes were full of trouble, but not of tears. With a quick, unconscious, supplicating gesture she turned and fled from the room.

A few minutes later, when Lady Bligh followed her, she said, very briefly and independently, that she was fatigued, and would come down no more. And so her first evening in England passed over.

IV

A Taste of Her Quality

Mr. Justice Bligh was an inveterate and even an irreclaimable early riser. In the pleasant months at Twickenham he became worse in this respect than ever, and it was no unusual thing for the slow summer dawns to find this eminent judge, in an old tweed suit, and with a silver frost upon his cheeks and chin, pottering about the stables, or the garden, or the river's brim.

The morning following the arrival of the happy pair, however, is scarcely a case in point, for it was fully six when Sir James sat down in his dressing-room to be shaved by his valet, the sober and vigilant Mr. Dix. This operation, for obvious reasons, was commonly conducted in dead silence; nor was the Judge ever very communicative with his servants; so that the interlude which occurred this morning was remarkable in itself, quite apart from what happened afterwards.

A series of loud reports of the nature of fog-signals had come suddenly through the open window, apparently from some part of the premises. The Judge held up his finger to stop the shaving.

"What is that noise, Dix?"

"Please, Sir James, it sounds like some person a-cracking of a whip, Sir James."

"A whip! I don't think so at all. It is more like pistol-shooting. Go to the window and see if you can see anything."

"No, Sir James, I can't see nothing at all," said Dix from the window; "but it do seem to come from the stable-yard, please, Sir James."

"I never heard a whip cracked like that," said the Judge. "Dear me, how it continues! Well, never mind; lather me afresh, Dix."

So the shaving went on; but in the stable-yard a fantastic scene was in full play. Its origin was in the idle behaviour of the stable-boy, who had interrupted his proper business of swilling the yard to crack a carriage-whip, by way of cheap and indolent variety. Now you cannot crack any kind of whip well without past practice and present pains; but this lad, who was of a mean moral calibre, had neither the character to practise nor the energy to take pains in anything. He cracked his whip as he did all things—execrably; and, when his wrist was suddenly and firmly seized from behind, the shock served the young ruffian right. His jaw dropped. "The devil!" he gasped; but, turning round, it appeared that he had made a mistake—unless, indeed, the devil had taken the form of a dark and beautiful young lady, with bright contemptuous eyes that made the lad shrivel and hang his head.

"Anyway, *you* can't crack a whip!" said the Bride, scornfully—for of course it was no one else.

The lad kept a sulky silence. The young lady picked up the whip that had fallen from his unnerved fingers. She looked very fresh and buoyant in the fresh summer morning, and very lovely. She could not have felt real fatigue the night before, for there was not a lingering trace of it in her appearance now; and if she had been really tired, why be up and out so very early this morning? The stable-boy began to glance at her furtively and to ask himself this last question, while Gladys handled and examined the whip in a manner indicating that she had handled a whip before.

"Show you how?" she asked suddenly; but the lad only dropped his eyes and shuffled his feet, and became a degree more sulky than before. Gladys stared at him in astonishment. She was new to England, and had yet to discover that there is a certain type of lout—a peculiarly English type—that infinitely prefers to be ground under heel by its betters to being treated with the least approach to freedom or geniality on their part. This order of being would resent the familiarity of an Archbishop much more bitterly than his Grace would resent the vilest abuse of the lout. It combines the touchiness of the sensitive-plant with the soul of the weed; and it was the Bride's first introduction to the variety—which, indeed, does not exist in Australia. She cracked the whip prettily, and with a light heart, and the boy glowered upon her. The exercise pleased her, and brought a dull red glow into her dusky cheeks, and heightened and set off her beauty, so that even the lout gaped at her with a sullen sense of satisfaction. Then, suddenly, she threw down the whip at his feet.

"*Take* the beastly thing!" she cried. "It isn't half a whip! But you just hold on, and I'll show you what a real whip is!"

She was out of the yard in a twinkling. The lout rubbed his eyes, scratched his head, and whistled. Then a brilliant idea struck him: he fetched the coachman. They were just in time. The Bride was back in a moment.

"Ha! two of you, eh?" she exclaimed. "Well, stand aside and I'll show you how we crack stock-whips in the Bush!"

A short, stout handle, tapering towards the lash, and no longer than fifteen inches, was in her hand. They could not see the lash at first, because she held it in front of her in her left hand, and it was of the same colour as her dark tailor-made dress; but the Bride jerked her right wrist gently, and then a thing like an attenuated brown snake, twelve feet long, lay stretched upon the wet cement of the yard as if by magic. Swiftly then she raised her arm, and the two spectators felt a fine line of water strike their faces as the lash came up from the wet cement; looking up, they saw a long black streak undulating for an instant above the young lady's head, and then they heard a whiz, followed by an almost deafening report. The lash lay on the ground again, quivering. Coachman and stable-boy instinctively flattened their backs against the coach-house door.

"That," said the Bride, "is the plain thing. Smell this!"

Again the long lash trembled over her head; again it cracked like a gun-shot somewhere in front of her, but this time, by the help of the recoil and by the sheer strength of her wrist, the lash darted out again behind her—as it seemed, under her very arm—and let out the report of a second barrel in the rear. And this fore-and-aft recoil cracking went on without intermission for at least a minute—that minute during which the Judge's shaving was interrupted. Then it stopped, and there was a fine wild light in the Bride's eyes, and her breath came quickly, and her lips and cheeks were glowing crimson.

The phlegmatic lad was quite speechless, and, in fact, with his gaping mouth and lolling tongue he presented a rather cruel spectacle. But the coachman found an awestruck word or two: "My soul and body!" he gasped.

"Ah!" said the Bride, "that *is* something flash, ain't it though? I wonder I hadn't forgotten it. And now *you* have a try, old man!"

Honest Garrod, the coachman, opened his eyes wide. He knew that this was Mrs. Alfred; he had heard that Mrs. Alfred was an Australian; but he could scarcely believe his ears.

"No, miss—no, mum—thank you," he faltered. The "miss" came much more naturally than the "mum."

"Come on!" cried the Bride.

"I'd rather not, miss—*mum*," said the coachman.

"What rot!" said Gladys. "Here—that's it—bravo! *Now* blaze away!"

The old man had given in, simply because this extraordinary young lady was irresistible. The first result of his weakness was a yell of pain from the stable-boy; the poor lad's face was bleeding where the lash had struck it. Rough apologies followed. Then the old coachman—who was not without mettle, and was on it, for the moment—took off his coat and tried again. After many futile efforts, however, he only succeeded in coiling the lash tightly round his own legs; and that made an end of it; the old man gave it up.

"Show us some more, mum," said he. "I've got too old and stiff for them games,"—as if in his youth he had been quite at home with the stock-whip, and only of late years had got rusty in the art of cracking it.

"Right you are," said Gladys, gaily, when her laughter was over—she had a hearty, but a rather musical laugh. "Give me the whip. Now, have you got a coin—a sixpence? No? No odds, here's half a sov. in my purse that'll do as well; and you shall have it, either of you that do this side o' Christmas what I'm going to do now. I'm going to show you a trick and a half!"

Her eyes sparkled with excitement: she was rather over-excited, perhaps. She placed the coin upon the ground, retreated several paces, measured the distance with her eye, and smartly raised the handle of the stock-whip. The crack that followed was the plain, straightforward crack, only executed with greater precision than before. Then she had resembled nothing so much as an angler idly flogging a stream; the difference was that now, as it were, she was throwing at a rise. And she threw with wonderful skill; for, at the first crack, the half-sovereign spun high into the air and fell with a ring upon the cement; she had picked it up on the point of the lash!

It was a surprising feat. That she managed to accomplish it at the first attempt surprised no one so much as the Bride herself. This also added in a dangerous degree to her excitement. She was now in little less than a frenzy. She seemed to forget where she was, and to think that she was back on the station in New South Wales, where she could do what she liked.

"Now that you've seen I can do that," she cried to the lad, "stand you with your back to the wall there, and I'll take your hat off for you!"

The answer of the dull youth was astonishingly wise; he said nothing at all, but beat a hasty retreat into the safety of the saddle-room.

She turned to the trembling Garrod. "Then you!"

Even as he demurred, he saw her hand go up. Next moment the whipcord hissed past his face and there was a deafening report in his right ear, and the next a fearful explosion just under his left ear, and many more at every turn and corner of his face, while the poor man stood with closed eyes and unuttered prayers. It was an elaborate substitute for the simpler fun of whipping his cap off, the unhappy creature being bareheaded already. At last, feeling himself still untouched, Garrod opened his eyes, watched his opportunity, and, while the lash still quivered in mid-air, turned and made a valiant bolt for shelter. His shirt was cut between the shoulder-blades as cleanly as though a knife had done it, but he reached the saddle-room with a whole skin.

"Ye cowardly devils!" roared the Bride, now beside herself—her dark eyes ablaze with diabolical merriment. "I'll keep you there all day, so help me, if you don't come out of it!" And, in the execution of her threat, the long lash cracked in the doorway with terrifying echoes.

At that moment, wildly excited as she was, she became conscious of a new presence in the yard. She turned her head, to see a somewhat mean-looking figure in ancient tweed, with his back to the light, but apparently regarding her closely from under the shadow of his broad felt wideawake.

"Another of 'em, I do declare!" cried the Bride. And with that the lash cracked in the ears of the unfortunate new-comer, who stood as though turned to stone.

The blue sky, from this luckless person's point of view, became alive with the writhings of serpents, hell-black and numberless. His ears were filled and stunned with the fiendish musketry. He stood like a statue; his hands were never lifted from the pockets of his Norfolk jacket; he never once removed his piercing gaze from the wild face of his tormentor.

"Why don't you take off your hat to a lady?" that lunatic now shouted, laughing hoarsely, but never pausing in her vile work. "Faith, but I'll do it for you!"

The wideawake then and there spun up into the air, even as the half-sovereign had spun before it. And the very next instant the stock-whip slipped from the fingers of the Bride. She had uncovered the gray hairs of her father-in-law, Sir James Bligh! At the same moment there was a loud shout behind her, and she staggered backward almost into the arms of her horror-stricken husband. Even then the Bride knew that Granville was there too, watching her misery with grinning eyes. And the Judge did not move a muscle, but stood as he had stood under her fire, piercing her through and through with his stern eyes; and there was an expression upon his face which the worst malefactors he had ever dealt with had perhaps not seen there; and a terrible silence held the air after the mad uproar of the last few minutes.

That awful stillness was broken by the patter of unsteady footsteps. With a crimson face the Bride tottered rather than ran across the yard, and fell upon her knees on the wet cement, at the Judge's feet.

"Forgive me," she said; "I never saw it was you!"

V

GRANVILLE ON THE SITUATION

It was in the forenoon of the same day that Granville entered abruptly his mother's sanctum. Lady Bligh was busily writing at the great office-table, but she looked up at once and laid down her pen. Granville threw himself into her easiest chair with an air of emancipation.

"They have gone!" he ejaculated. If he had referred to the British workman or to the bailiffs he could not have employed more emphatic tones of relief; so Lady Bligh naturally asked to whom he did refer.

"To the happy pair!" said Granville.

"They have gone to town, then?"

"To town for the day."

Lady Bligh took up her pen again, but only to wipe it, deliberately. "Now, Granville," she said, leaning back in her chair, "I want you to tell me the truth about—about whatever happened before breakfast. I don't know yet quite what did happen. I want to get at the truth; but so far I have been able to gather only shreds and patches of the truth."

Granville rose briskly to his feet and took his stand upon the hearthrug. Then he leant an elbow on the chimney-piece, adjusted his eyeglass, and smiled down upon Lady Bligh. One easily might have imagined that the task imposed upon him was congenial in the extreme. Without further pressing he told the story, and told it succinctly and well, with a zest that was vaguely felt rather than detected, and with an entire and artistic suppression of his usual commentaries. The mere story was so effective in itself that the most humorous parenthesis could not have improved it, and Granville had the wit to tell it simply. But when he reached the point where the Judge appeared on the scene Lady Bligh stopped him; Granville was disappointed.

"I think perhaps I have been told what happened then," said Lady Bligh; "at all events I seem to know, and I don't care to hear it again. Oh! it was too scandalous! But tell me, Gran, how did your father bear it?—at the time, I mean."

"Like a man!" said Granville, with righteous warmth. "Like a man! With that vile whip cracking under his very nose, he did not flinch—he did not stir. Then she whipped his hat from his head; and then she saw what she had done, and went down on her knees to him—as if *that* would undo it!"

"And your father?"

"My father behaved splendidly; as no other man in England in his position and—in *that* position—would have behaved. He told her at once, when she said she had not seen it was he, that he quite understood that; that, in fact, he had seen it for himself from the first. Then he told her to get up that instant; then he smiled—actually smiled; and then— you will hardly believe this, but it is a fact—he gave his arm to Mistress Gladys and took her in to breakfast!"

Lady Bligh sighed, but made no remark.

"It was more than she deserved; even Alfred admitted that."

Lady Bligh did not answer.

"Even Alfred was knocked out of time. I never saw a fellow look more put out than he did at breakfast. He had warned us to prepare for 'mannerisms,' but—"

Granville made a tempting pause. Lady Bligh, however, refused to fill it in. She was engrossed in thought. Her line of thought suddenly flashed across Granville, and he caught it up dexterously.

"As for the Judge," said he, "what the Judge feels no one can say. As I said, he behaved as only he could have behaved in the infamous circumstances. But I did see him steal a quiet glance at Alfred; and that glance said plainer than words: '*You've* done it, my boy; this is irrevocable!'"

Lady Bligh was drawn at last.

"This is very painful," she murmured; "this is too painful, Granville!"

"Painful?" cried Granville. "I grant you it's painful; but it's the fact; it's got to be faced."

"That may be," said Lady Bligh, sadly; "that may be. But we ought not to be hasty; and we certainly ought not to make too much of this one escapade."

Granville shook his head wisely, and smiled.

"I don't think there is much fear of *that*. On the contrary, I doubt if our eyes are even yet fully open to the enormity of this morning's work. I don't think we any of us realise the hideous indignity to which my father has been subjected. But we should. We should think of it—and of him. Here we have one of the oldest and ablest of Her Majesty's judges—a man of the widest experience and of the fairest fame, whose name is a synonym for honour and humanity, not only in the Profession, but throughout every section of the community—a man, my dear mother, with whom the very smartest of us—I tell you frankly—would fight shy of a tilt in court, yet whom we all respect and honour; in very truth, 'a wise and upright judge,' though I say it who am his son. And what has happened to him? How has he been treated?" cried Granville. "Well, we know. No need to go into that again. Only *try* to realise it, dear mother; try to realise it. To me there is, I confess, something almost epic in this business!"

"I don't wish to realise it; and I don't know, I am sure, why you should wish to make me."

"For no reason," said Granville, shrugging his shoulders, and also looking hurt; "for no kind of reason, except that it *did* strike me that my father's character had never—never, that is, in his home life—come out more strongly or more generously. Why, I should like to lay ruinous odds that he never refers to the matter again, even to you; while, you shall see, his manner to her will not suffer the slightest change in consequence of what has happened."

"It would be a terrible thing if it did," said Lady Bligh; and she added after a pause: "She *is* so beautiful!"

Granville drummed with his fingers upon the chimney-piece. His mother wanted a reply. She wanted sympathy upon this point; it was a very insignificant point, the Bride's personal beauty; but as yet it seemed to be the only redeeming feature in Alfred's unfortunate marriage.

"You can't deny *that*, Gran?" she persisted.

"Deny what? The young woman's prepossessing appearance? Certainly not; nobody with eyes to see could deny that."

"And after all," said Lady Bligh, "brought up as she evidently has been, it would be astonishing indeed if her ways were *not* wild and strange. Consequently, Gran, there is every hope that she will fall into our ways very soon; is there not?"

"Oh, of course there is *hope*," said Gran, with an emphasis that was the reverse of hopeful; "and there is hope, too, that she will ultimately fall into our way of speaking: her own 'mannerisms,' in that respect, are just a little too marked. Oh, yes, there is hope; there is hope."

Lady Bligh said no more; she seemed to have no more to say. Observing this, Granville consulted his watch, said something about an engagement in town, and went to the door.

"Going to London?" said Lady Bligh. "You might have gone with them, I think."

"I think not," said Granville. "I should have been out of place. They were going to Madame Tussaud's, or the Tower of London, or the Zoological Gardens—I don't know which—perhaps to all three. But the Bride will tell us all about it this evening and how the sights of London compare with the sights of Melbourne; we may look forward to that; and, till then—good-bye."

So Lady Bligh was once more alone. She did not at once resume her correspondence, however. Leaning back in her chair, she gazed thoughtfully through the open window at her side, and across the narrow lawn to where the sunlit river was a silver band behind the trunks and nether foliage of the trees. Lady Bligh was sad, and no wonder; but in her heart was little of the wounded pride, and none of the personal bitterness, that many mothers would feel—and do feel every day—under similar circumstances. What were the circumstances? Simply these: her eldest son had married a wife who was beautiful, it was true, and good-tempered, it appeared; but one who was, on the other hand, both vulgar and ignorant, and, as a daughter, in every way impossible. These hard words Lady Bligh pronounced deliberately in her mind. She was facing the fact, as Granville had said that it should be faced. Yet Granville had used no such words as these; if he had, he would have been given reason to regret them.

For, as has been said already, Lady Bligh had a tolerably just estimate of her son Granville; she thought him only rather more clever, and a good deal more good-natured, than he really was. She knew that a man of any cleverness at all is fond of airing his cleverness—and, indeed, must air it—particularly if he is a young man. For this reason, she made it a rule to listen generously to all Granville had to say to her. But there was another reason: Lady Bligh was a woman who valued highly the confidence and companionship of her sons. Sometimes, it is true, she thought Granville's cynicism both cheap and worthless; and sometimes (though more rarely) she told him so. Often she thought him absurd: she was amused, for instance, when he solemnly assured her of the Judge's high standing and fair fame in "the Profession"—as if she needed *his* assurance on that point! But it very seldom seemed to her that the things he said were really ill-natured. There, in the main, she was right. There was no downright malice (as a rule) in Granville; he was merely egotistical and vain; he merely loved more than most things the sound of his own voice. He did not designedly make unkind remarks—at least, not often; but he never took any pains to make kind ones. He passed among men for a fellow of good nature, and unquestionably he was good company. Certainly Lady Bligh overestimated his good nature; but to a great extent she understood Granville; and in any case—of course—she loved him. But she loved Alfred more; and it was Alfred who had made this marriage.

Yet it was only with grief that she could think of the marriage, at present; she found it impossible to harbour bitter feeling against the young handsome face and honest brave eyes that had taken poor Alfred by storm, though they had blinded him to a hundred blemishes. The fact is, her daughter-in-law's face was haunting Lady Bligh. As the day wore on she found herself longing wistfully to see it again. When she did see it again, the face was changed; its expression was thoughtful, subdued, and even sad. Nor were there any *gaucheries* at dinner that night, for both Alfred and Gladys were silent and constrained in manner.

Then Lady Bligh took heart afresh.

"It *is* only her bringing up," she said. "She will fall into our ways in time; indeed, she is falling into them already—though not in the way I wish her to; for it must not make her sad, and it must not make her feel ashamed. It shall not; for I mean to help her. I mean to be to her what, indeed, I already am without choice—her mother—if she will only let me!"

VI

COMPARING NOTES

B ut, during those first few days, Lady Bligh did not get many opportunities of carrying out her good intentions towards her daughter-in-law. For several mornings in succession Alfred carried off his wife to London, and they never returned until late in the afternoon, while twice during the first week the pair went to the theatre. They were seeing the sights of the town; and the Bride did appear to be impressed with what she saw; but the prospect of an unreserved and racy commentary upon everything, which the first hour of her installation in her husband's family had seemed to hold out—and which Granville, for one, had counted upon—was not properly realised. And at this Alfred perhaps, was scarcely less disappointed than Granville.

"Why don't you tell them more what you think of things?" said Alfred. "They won't fancy you half appreciate the Old Country."

"I can't help it," replied his young wife. "You know that I *do* like what I see, dear: you know that I am just delighted with everything: but how can I tell them so, unless I tell them in my own way? Well, then, I see they don't like it when I drag in the Colonies; yet you must compare what you see with something you've seen before; and the Colonies is the only other country ever I did see."

But the fact is, it was not so much their daughter-in-law's comparisons, which were inoffensive in themselves, as the terms in which these comparisons were expressed, that Lady Bligh and Sir James felt bound to discourage. For it soon became plain that Gladys could not talk for two minutes about her native country without unseemly excitement; and this excitement was invariably accompanied by a small broadside of undesirable phrases, and by an aggravation of the dreadful Australian twang, even if some quite indecorous Bush idiom did not necessitate a hasty change of subject. When Australia was rigorously tabooed the Bride was safe, and stupid; when it was not, she might be bright and animated and amusing—but you could never tell what she would say next—the conversation was full of perils and pitfalls.

The particular conversations that revealed the thinness of the ice in this quarter were trivial in the extreme. In them it was mere touch-and-go with the dangerous subject, nothing more: nothing more because Gladys was quick to perceive that the subject was unpopular. So she became rather silent in the long evenings at the dinner-table and in the drawing-room; for it was her only subject, this one that they did not seem to like. To strangers, however, who were glad to get up a conversation with one of the prettiest women they had ever met in their lives, this seemed the likeliest topic in the world; *they* could not know that Australia was dangerous ground. The first of them who ventured upon it did not soon forget the experience; it was probably always a more amusing reminiscence to him than to Gladys's new relatives, who heard all that passed, and grinned and bore it.

The stranger in question was by way of being illustrious. He was a Midland magnate, and his name, Travers, was a good one; but, what was for the moment much more to the point, he was a very newly elected Member of the House of Commons; in fact, "the new boy" there. He came down to dinner at Twickenham flushed with the agreeable heat of successful battle. Only the week before he had snatched his native borough from the spreading fire of Democracy, and won one of the very closest and most keenly contested by-elections of that year. Naturally enough, being a friend of some standing, he talked freely of his electioneering experiences, and with a victor's rightful relish. His manner, it must be owned, was a trifle ponderous; according to Granville, he was an inflated bore. But Mr. Travers, M.P., was sufficiently well listened to (Lady Bligh was such a wonderful listener); and he fought his good fight over and over again with such untiring energy, and depicted it from so many commanding points of view, that, even when it came to tea in the drawing-room, the subject was still unfinished. At all events, it then for the first time became lively; for it was then that Mr. Travers turned to young Mrs. Bligh (also for the first time), and honoured her with an observation:—

"No doubt you order these things better in Australia; eh?"

"What things?" asked the Bride, with some eagerness; for of Australia she had been thinking, but not of Mr. Travers or his election.

"Why," said the Member, with dignity, "your elections. I was speaking of the difficulty of getting some of the lower orders to the poll; you have almost to drive them there. What I say is, that very probably, in Australia, you manage these things on a superior system."

"We do," said the Bride laconically.

The new Member looked astonished; he had expected a more modest answer.

"Indeed!" he said stiffly, and addressed himself to his tea-cup.

"For," explained the Bride, exhibiting dangerous symptoms, "we *do* drive 'em to the poll out there, and make no bones about it either!"

"Indeed?" said Mr. Travers again; but this time there was some curiosity in his tone. "This is interesting. I always thought Australia was such a superlatively *free* country!"

The Bride scented a sarcasm.

"So it is," she cried warmly, beginning to speak at a perilous pace, and with her worst twang; "*my* word it is! But you don't understand me. It's like this: we *do* drive 'em to the poll, up the Bush; I've driven 'em lots o' times myself. They're camped out—the voters, like—all over the runs, for all the hands have a vote; and to get 'em to the police-barracks (the poll, d'ye see?) on election day, each squatter's got to muster his own men and drive 'em in. I used to take one trap with four horses, and father another. Gracious, what a bit of fun it was! But the difficulty was—"

She hesitated, for Lady Bligh was staring at her; and, though her ladyship's face was in shadow, the Bride was disturbed, for a moment, by the rigid pose of the old lady's head. A queer expression was come over the face of the new Member, moreover; but this Gladys could not see, for he was a tall man, standing, while she was seated.

"What *was* the difficulty?" asked Granville from a corner, in an encouraging tone.

Gladys instantly forgot Lady Bligh. "To keep 'em from going to the shanty *first*," she answered, with a merry laugh.

"The shanty?" repeated Mr. Travers, with a vague idea of sailors' songs.

"The pub., then. Of course they all went afterwards, and—but we were obliged to keep them sober till they'd voted; and that's where the difficulty came in."

The assembly shuddered; but, before new ground could be broken, Mr. Travers, for the first time interested in somebody else's electioneering experiences, said inquiringly:—

"These squatters I presume, represent the landed interest; *my* party, in fact?"

"Oh, I don't know nothing about that," replied the Bride.

At this juncture Alfred announced, in an uncommonly loud and aggressive tone, that—what do you think?—the glass was going down!

"Is it?" cried Sir James, with a lively concern quite foreign to his habit. "Dear, dear! And Mr. Travers just now assured me that the weather was quite settled. I fear that this will disappoint—er—Mr. Travers!"

But it failed even to attract that gentleman's attention; and Granville, in the background, chuckled satanically over the ingenuousness of the device. Mr. Travers, in fact, was sufficiently interested elsewhere. "Yet, of course," he was saying, "there *are* two parties?"

"*My* word, there are!" returned the Bride.

"And do you call them Whig and Tory?"

"I don't think it"—doubtfully.

"Conservative and Liberal, perhaps?"

"Not that I know of."

"Yet you say you have two parties—"

"Of course we have, same as you," broke in the Bride, who would brook anything rather than the implied inferiority of Australia in the most trivial respect. "But all ever *I* heard 'em called was the squatters' candidate and the selectors' *man!*"

"And your men, I suppose, voted for the squatters' candidate?"

"I should rather hope so!" said Mrs. Alfred, with severe emphasis. "Even Daft Larry—who's both deaf and mad—had sense enough to give us his vote!"

Mr. Travers, though astonished at her tone, said nothing at the moment; but Granville asked from his corner:—

"What if they didn't, Gladys?"

The Bride was seized with a sudden fit of uncontrollable mirth. Some reminiscence evidently tickled her.

"There *was* one man that we knew of that voted wrong," she said, "and he got it pretty hot, I can tell you!"

"Advanced Australia!" murmured Granville.

"I am sorry to hear that, Mrs. Bligh," said Mr. Travers (who had ceased to deal with those local tradesmen, at his place in the Midlands, who were suspected of having "voted wrong" the previous week). "I am sorry indeed to hear that. May I ask who punished him?"

"Certainly—*I* did."

It was a startling reply. The Judge quietly quitted the room. Alfred, with his back to every one, surveyed his red face in the mantel-mirror, and ground his teeth; only Lady Bligh sat stoically still.

"He came back to the trap very drunk—blind, speechless, paralytic," the Bride explained rapidly, "and owned up what he'd done as bold as brass. So I let him have it with the whip, pretty sudden, I can tell you. It was chiefly for his drunken insolence—but not altogether," said Gladys, candidly.

Mr. Travers had been glad to pick up a thing or two concerning Australian politics, but he seemed now to consider himself sufficiently enlightened.

"Do you sing, Mrs. Bligh?" he asked somewhat abruptly.

"Not a note," said the Bride, perceiving with regret that the subject was changed.

"You play, perhaps? If so—"

"No, I can't play neither," said the Bride, smiling broadly—and bewitchingly. "I'm no good at all, you see!"

It seemed too true. She had not the saving grace of a single accomplishment—nothing, nothing, nothing but her looks!

VII

In Richmond Park

The day after Mr. Travers dined at Twickenham was almost the first day that passed without the happy pair running up to London together.

"It's far too hot to think of town, or of wearing anything but flannels all day," said Alfred in the morning. "But there's plenty to see hereabouts, Gladdie. There's Bushey Park and Hampton Court, and Kew Gardens, and Richmond Park. What do you say to a stroll in Richmond Park? It's as near as anything, and we shall certainly get most air there."

Gladys answered promptly that she was "on" (they were alone); and they set out while the early haze of a sweltering day was hanging closely over all the land, but closest of all about the river.

There was something almost touching in the air of serious responsibility with which these two went about their daily sight-seeing; though Granville derived the liveliest entertainment from the spectacle. The worst of guides himself, and in many respects the least well-informed of men, Alfred nevertheless had no notion of calling in the aid of a better qualified cicerone, and of falling into the rear himself to listen and learn with his wife. At the same time, the fierce importance, to his wife, of this kind of education exaggerated itself in his mind; so he secretly armed himself with "Baedeker," and managed to keep a lesson ahead of his pupil, on principles well known to all who have ever dabbled in the noble art of "tutoring." But, indeed, Alfred's whole conduct towards his wife was touching—touching in its perpetual tenderness, touching in its unflagging consideration, and ten times touching in the fact that his devotion was no longer blind. His eyes had been slowly and painfully opened during this first week at home. Peculiar manners, which, out there in the Bush, had not been peculiar, seemed worse than that here in England. They had to bear continual comparison with the soft speech and gentle ways of Lady Bligh, and the contrast was sharp and cruel. But the more Alfred realised his wife's defects the more he loved her. That was the nature of his simple heart and its simple love. At least *she* should not know that he saw her in a different light, and at first he would have cut his tongue out rather than tell her plainly of her peculiarities. Presently she would see them for herself, and then, in her own good time, she would rub down of her own accord the sharper angles; and then she would take Lady Bligh for her model, instinctively, without being told to do so: and so all would be well. Arguing thus, Alfred had not allowed her to say a word to him about that escapade with the stock-whip on the first morning, for her penitence was grievous to him—and was it a thing in the least likely to happen twice? Nevertheless, he was thoroughly miserable in a week—that electioneering conversation was the finisher—and at last he had determined to speak. Thus the walk to Richmond was strangely silent, for all the time he was casting about for some way of expressing what was in his mind, without either wounding her feelings or letting her see that his own were sore.

Now they walked to Richmond by the river, and then over the bridge, but, before they climbed the hill to the park gates, a solemn ceremony, insisted upon by Alfred, was duly observed: the Bride ate a "Maid-of-Honour" in the Original Shop; and when the famous delicacy had been despatched and criticised, and Alfred had given a wild and stumbling account of its historic origin, his wife led the way back into the sunshine in such high spirits that his own dejection deepened sensibly as the burden of his unuttered remonstrances increased. At last, in despair, he resolved to hold his tongue, for that morning at least. Then, indeed, they chatted cheerfully together for the first time during the walk, and he was partly with her in her abuse of the narrow streets and pavements of Richmond, but still stuck up for them on the plea that they were quaint and thoroughly English; whereat she laughed him to scorn; and so they reached the park.

But no sooner was the soft cool grass under their dusty feet, and the upland swelling before them as far as the eye could travel, than the Bride became suddenly and unaccountably silent. Alfred stole curious glances as he walked at her side, and it seemed to him that the dark eyes roving so eagerly over the landscape were grown wistful and sad.

"How like it is to the old place!" she exclaimed at last.

"You don't mean your father's run, Gladdie?"

"Yes, I do; this reminds me of it more than anything I've seen yet."

"What nonsense, my darling!" said Alfred, laughing. "Why, there is no such green spot as this in all Australia!"

"Ah! you were there in the drought, you see; you never saw the run after decent rains. If you had, you'd soon see the likeness between those big paddocks in what we call the 'C Block' and this. But the road spoils this place; it wants a Bush road; let's get off it for a bit."

So they bore inward, to the left, and Gladys was too thoroughly charmed, and too thoughtful, to say much. And now the cool bracken was higher than their knees, and the sun beat upon their backs very fiercely; and now they walked upon turf like velvet, in the shadow of the trees.

"You don't get many trees like these out there," said Alfred.

"Well—not in Riverina, I know we don't," Gladys reluctantly admitted; and soon she added: "Nor any water-holes like this."

For they found themselves on the margin of the largest of the Pen Ponds. There was no wind, not a ripple could be seen upon the whole expanse of the water. The fierce sun was still mellowed by a thin, gauzy haze, and the rays were diffused over the pond in a solid gleam. The trees on the far side showed fairly distinct outlines, filled in with a bluish smoky gray, and entirely without detail. The day was sufficiently sultry, even for the Thames Valley.

"And yet," continued Gladys, speaking slowly and thoughtfully, "it *does* remind one of the Bush, somehow. I have sometimes brought a mob of sheep through the scrub to the water, in the middle of the day, and the water has looked just like this—like a great big lump of quicksilver pressed into the ground and shaved off level. That'd be on the hot still days, something like to-day. We now and then did have a day like this, you know—only, of course, a jolly sight hotter. But we had more days with the hot wind, hot and strong; what terrors they were when you were driving sheep!"

"You were a tremendous stock-rider, Gladdie!" remarked her husband.

"Wasn't I just! Ever since I was *that* high! And I was fond, like, of that old run—knew every inch of it better than any man on the place—except the old man, and perhaps Daft Larry. Knew it, bless you! from sunrise—you remember the sunrise out there, dull, and red, and sudden—to sundown, when you spotted the station pines black as ink against the bit of pink sky, as you came back from mustering. Let's see—I forget how it goes—no, it's like this:—

"'Twas merry 'mid the black-woods when we spied the station roofs,
To wheel the wild scrub cattle at the yard,
With a running fire of stock-whips and a fiery run of hoofs,
Oh, the hardest day was never then too hard!

That's how it goes, I think. We used sometimes to remember it as we rode home, dog-tired. But it was sheep with us, not cattle, more's the pity. Why, what's wrong, Alfred? Have you seen a ghost?"

"No. But you fairly amaze me, darling. I'd no idea you knew any poetry. What is it?"

"Gordon—mean to say you've never heard of him? Adam Lindsay Gordon! You *must* have heard of him, out there. *Everybody* knows him in the Bush. Why, I've heard shearers, and hawkers, and swagmen spouting him by the yard! He was our Australian poet, and *you* never had one to beat him. Father says so. Father says he is as good as Shakespeare."

Alfred made no contradiction, for a simple reason: he had not listened to her last sentences; he was thinking how well she hit off the Bush, and how nicely she quoted poetry. He was silent for some minutes. Then he said earnestly:—

"I wish, my darling, that you would sometimes talk to my mother like that!"

Gladys returned from the antipodes in a flash. "I shall never talk to any of your people any more about Australia!" And, by her tone, she meant it.

"Why not?"

"Because they don't like it, Alfred; I see they don't, though I never see it so clearly as when it's all over and too late. Yet why should they hate it so? Why should it annoy them? I've nothing else to talk about, and I should have thought they'd like to hear of another country. I know *I* liked to hear all about England from *you*, Alfred!"

Faint though it was, the reproach in her voice cut him to the heart. Yet his moment had come. He had decided, it is true, to say nothing at all; but then there had been no opening, and here was one such as might never come again.

"Gladdie," he began, with great tenderness, "don't be hurt, but I'm going to tell you what *may* have something to do with it. You know, you are apt to get—I won't say excited—but perhaps a little *too* enthusiastic, when you talk of the Bush. Quite right—and no wonder, *I* say—but then, here in England, somehow, they very seldom seem to get enthusiastic. Then, again—I think—perhaps—you say things that are all right out there, but sound odd in our ridiculous ears. For we are an abominable, insular nation of humbugs—" began poor Alfred with a tremendous burst of indignation, fearing that he had said too much, and making a floundering effort to get out of what he *had* said. But his wife cut him short.

The colour had mounted to her olive cheeks. Denseness, at all events, was not among her failings—when she kept calm.

She was sufficiently calm now. "I see what you mean, and I shall certainly say no more about Australia. 'I like a man that is well-bred!' Do you remember how Daft Larry used to wag his head and say that whenever he saw you? 'You're not one of the low sort,' he used to go on; and how we did laugh! But I've been thinking, Alfred, that he couldn't have said the same about me, if I'd been a man. And—and that's at the bottom of it all!" She smiled, but her smile was sad.

"You are offended, Gladys?"

"Not a bit. Only I seem to understand."

"You *don't* understand! And that *isn't* at the bottom of it!"

"Very well, then, it isn't. So stop frowning like that this instant. I'd no idea you looked so well when you were fierce. I shall make you fierce often now. Come, you stupid boy! I shall learn in time. How do you know I'm not learning already? Come away; we've had enough of the water-hole, I think."

She took his arm, and together they struck across to Ham Gate. But Alfred was silent and moody; and the Bride knew why.

"*Dear* old Alfred," she said at last, pressing his arm with her hand; "I *know* I shall get on well with all your people, in time."

"All of them, Gladdie?"

"At any rate, all but Granville."

"Still not Gran! I was afraid of it."

"No; I shall never care much about Gran. I can't help it, really I can't. He is everlastingly sneering, and he thinks himself so much smarter than he is. Then he enjoys it when I make a fool of myself; I see he does; and—oh, I can't bear him!"

A pugnacious expression came into Alfred's face, but passed over, and left it only stern.

"Yes," he said, "I know his infernal manner; but, when he sneers, it's only to show what a superior sort of fellow he is; he doesn't mean anything by it. The truth is, I fear he's becoming a bit of a snob; but at least he's a far better fellow than you think; there really isn't a better fellow going. Take my word for it, and for Heaven's sake avoid words with *him*; will you promise me this much, Gladdie?"

"Very well—though I *have* once or twice thought there'd be a row between us, and though I *do* think what he'd hear from me would do him all the good in the world. But I promise. And I promise, too, not to gas about Australia, to any of them for a whole week. So there."

They walked on, almost in silence, until Ham Common was crossed and they had reached the middle of the delightful green. And here—with the old-fashioned houses on three sides of them, and the avenue of elms behind them and the most orthodox of village duck-ponds at their feet—Gladys stopped short, and fairly burst into raptures.

"But," said Alfred, as soon as he could get a word in, which was not immediately, "you go on as though this was the first real, genuine English village you'd seen; whereas nothing could be more entirely and typically English than Twickenham itself."

"Ah, but this seems miles and miles away from Twickenham, and all the other villages round about that I've seen. I think I would rather live here, where it is so quiet and still, like a Bush township. I like Twickenham; but on one side there's nothing but people going up and down in boats, and on the other side the same thing, only coaches instead of boats. And I hate the sound of those coaches, with their jingle and rattle and horn-blowing; though I shouldn't hate it if I were on one."

"Would you so very much like to fizz around on a coach, then?"

"Would I *not*!" said Gladys.

The first person they saw, on getting home, was Granville, who was lounging in the little veranda where they had taken tea on the afternoon of their arrival, smoking cigarettes over a book. It was the first volume of a novel, which he was scanning for review. He seemed disposed to be agreeable.

"Gladys," he said, "this book's about Australia; what's a 'new chum,' please? I may as well know, as, so far, the hero's one."

"A 'new chum,'" his sister-in-law answered him readily, "is some fellow newly out from home, who goes up the Bush; and he's generally a fool."

"Thank you," said Granville; "the hero of this story answers in every particular to your definition."

Granville went on with his skimming. On a slip of paper lying handy were the skeletons of some of the smart epigrammatic sentences with which the book would presently be pulverised. Husband and wife had gone through into the house, leaving him to his congenial task; when the Tempter, in humorous mood, put it into the head of his good friend Granville to call back the Bride for a moment's sport.

"I say"—the young man assumed the air of the innocent interlocutor—"is it true that every one out there wears a big black beard, and a red shirt, and jack-boots and revolvers?"

"No, it is not; who says so?"

"Well, this fellow gives me that impression. In point of fact, it always *was* my impression. Isn't it a fact, however, that most of your legislators (I meant to ask you this last night, but our friend the senator gave me no chance)—that most of your legislators are convicts?"

"Does your book give you that impression too?" the Bride inquired coolly.

"No; that's original, more or less."

"Then it's wrong, altogether. But, see here, Gran: you ought to go out there."

"Why, pray?"

"You remember what I said a 'new chum' was?"

"Yes; among other things a fool."

"Very good. You ought to go out there, because there are the makings of such a splendid 'new chum' in *you*. You're thrown away in England."

Granville dropped his book and put up his eyeglass. But the Bride was gone. She had already overtaken her husband, and seized him by the arm.

"Oh, Alfred," she cried, "I have done it! I have broken my promise! I have had words with Gran! Oh, my poor boy—I'm beginning to make you wish to goodness you'd never seen me—I feel I am!"

VIII

GRAN'S REVENGE

All men may be vain, but the vanity of Granville Bligh was, so to speak, of a special brand. In the bandying of words (which, after all, was his profession) his vanity was not too easily satisfied by his own performances. This made him strong in attack, through setting up a high standard, of the kind; but it left his defence somewhat weak for want of practice. His war was always within the enemy's lines. He paid too much attention to his attack. Thus, though seldom touched by an adversary, when touched he was wounded; and, what was likely to militate against his professional chances, when wounded he was generally winged. His own skin was too thin; he had not yet learned to take without a twinge what he gave without a qualm: for a smart and aggressive young man he was simply absurdly sensitive.

But, though weaker in defence than might have been expected, Granville was no mean hand at retaliation. He neither forgot nor forgave; and he paid on old scores and new ones with the heavy interest demanded by his exorbitant vanity. Here again his vanity was very fastidious. First or last, by fair means or foul, Granville was to finish a winner. Until he did, his vanity and he were not on speaking terms.

There were occasions, of course, when he was not in a position either to *riposte* at once or to whet his blade and pray for the next merry meeting. Such cases occurred sometimes in court, when the bench would stand no nonsense, and brusquely said as much, if not rather more. Incredible as it may seem, however, Granville felt his impotency hardly less in the public streets, when he happened to be unusually well dressed and gutter-chaff rose to the occasion. In fact, probably the worst half-hour he ever spent in his life was one fine morning when unaccountable energy actuated him to walk to Richmond, and take the train there, instead of getting in at Twickenham; for, encountering a motley and interminable string of vehicles *en route* to Kempton Park, he ran a gauntlet of plebeian satire during that half-hour, such as he never entirely could forget.

To these abominable experiences, the Bride's piece of rudeness unrefined (which she had the bad taste to perpetrate at the very moment when he was being rude to her, but in a gentlemanlike way) was indeed a mere trifle; but Granville, it will now be seen, thought more of trifles than the ordinary rational animal; and this one completely altered his attitude towards Gladys.

If, hitherto, he had ridiculed her, delicately, to her face, and disparaged her—with less delicacy—behind her back, he had been merely pursuing a species of intellectual sport, without much malicious intent. He was not aware that he had ever made the poor thing uncomfortable. He had not inquired into that. He was only aware that he had more than once had his joke out of her, and enjoyed it, and felt pleased with himself. But his sentiment towards her was no longer so devoid of animosity. She had scored off him; he had felt it sufficiently at the moment; but he felt it much more when it had rankled a little. And he despised and detested himself for having been scored off, even without witnesses, by a creature so coarse and contemptible. He was too vain to satisfy himself with the comfortable, elastic, and deservedly popular principle that certain unpleasantnesses and certain unpleasant people are "beneath notice." Nobody was beneath Granville's notice; he would have punished with his own boot the young blackguards of the gutter, could he have been sure of catching them, and equally sure of not being seen; and he punished Gladys in a fashion that precluded detection—even Gladys herself never knew that she was under the lash.

On the contrary, she ceased to dislike her brother-in-law. He was become more polite to her than he had ever been before; more affable and friendly in every way. Quite suddenly, they were brother and sister together.

"How well those two get on!" Lady Bligh would whisper to her husband, during the solemn game of *bezique* which was an institution of their quieter evenings; and, indeed, the Bride and her brother-in-law had taken to talking and laughing a good deal in the twilight by the open window. But, sooner or later, Granville was sure to come over to the card-table with Gladys's latest story or saying, with which he would appear to be hugely amused: and the same he delighted to repeat in its original vernacular, and with its original slips of grammar, but with his own faultless accent—which emphasised those peculiarities, making Lady Bligh sigh sadly and Sir James look as though he did not hear. And Alfred was too well pleased that his wife had come to like Granville at last, to listen to what they were talking about; and the poor girl herself never once suspected the unkindness; far from it, indeed, for she liked Granville now.

"I thought he would never forgive me for giving him that bit of my mind the other day; but you see, Alfred, it did him good; and now I like him better than I ever thought possible in this world. He's awfully good to me. And we take an interest in the same sort of things. Didn't you hear how interested he was in Bella's sweetheart at lunch to-day?"

Alfred turned away from the fresh bright face that was raised to his. He could not repress a frown.

"I *do* wish you wouldn't call the girl Bella," he said, with some irritation. "Her name's Bunn. Why don't you *call* her Bunn, dear? And nobody dreams of making talk about their maids' affairs, let alone their maids' young men, at the table. It's not the custom—not in England."

A week ago he would not have remonstrated with her upon so small a matter; but the ice had been broken that morning in Richmond Park. And a week ago she would very likely have told him, laughingly, to hang his English customs; but now she looked both pained and puzzled, as she begged him to explain to her the harm in what she had said.

"Harm?" said Alfred, more tenderly. "Well, there was no real *harm* in it—that's the wrong word altogether—especially as we were by ourselves, without guests. Still, you know, the mother doesn't want to hear all about her servants' family affairs, and what her servants' sweethearts are doing in Australia, or anywhere else. All that—particularly when you talk of the woman by her Christian name—sounds very much— why, it sounds almost as though you made a personal friend of the girl, Gladdie!"

Gladys opened wide her lovely eyes. "Why, so I do!"

Alfred looked uncomfortable.

"So I do!" said the Bride again. "And why not, pray? There, you see, you know of no reason why I shouldn't be friends with her, you goose! But I won't speak of her any more as Bella, if you don't like—except to her face. I shall call her what I please to her face, sir! But, indeed, I wouldn't have spoken about her at all to-day, only I *was* interested to know her young man was out there; and Gran seemed as interested as me, for he went on asking questions—"

Alfred was quite himself again.

"Any way, darling," he said, interrupting her with a kiss, "I am glad you have got over your prejudice against Gran!"—and he went out, looking it; but leaving behind him less of gladness than he carried away.

The conversation had taken place in the little morning-room in the front of the house, which faced the west; and the strong afternoon sunshine, striking down through the trembling tree-tops, dappled the Bride's face with lights and shadows. It was not, at the moment, a very happy face. All the reckless, radiant, aggressive independence of two or three weeks ago was gone out of it. The bold, direct glance was somewhat less bold. The dark, lustrous, lovely eyes were become strangely wistful. Gladys was in trouble.

It had crept upon her by slow degrees. Shade by shade the fatal truth had dawned even upon her—the fatal disparity between herself and her new relatives. This was plainer to no one now than to the Bride herself; and to her the disparity meant despair—it was so wide—and it grew wider day by day, as her realisation of it became complete. Well, she had made friends with Granville: but that was all. The Judge had been distant and ceremonious from the first: he was distant and ceremonious still. He had never again unbent so much as at that tragic moment when he bade her rise from her knees in the wet stable-yard. As for Lady Bligh, she had begun by being kind enough; but her kindness had run to silent sadness. She seemed full of regrets. Gladys was as far from her as ever. And Gladys knew the reasons for all this—some of them. She saw, now, the most conspicuous among her own shortcomings; and against those that she did see (Heaven knows) she struggled strenuously. But there were many she could not see, yet; she felt this, vaguely; and it was this that filled her with despair.

It was green grass that she gazed out upon from the morning-room window, as the trouble deepened in her eyes; and in Australia she had seldom seen grass that was green. But just then she would have given all the meadows of England for one strip of dry saltbush plain, with the sun dropping down behind the far-away line of sombre, low-sized scrub, and the sand-hills flushing in the blood-red light, and the cool evening wind coming up from the south. The picture was very real to her—as real, for the moment, as this shaven grass-plot, and the line of tall trees that shadowed it, with their trunks indistinguishable, in this light, against the old brick wall. Then she sighed, and the vision vanished—and she thought of Alfred.

"He can't go on loving me always, unless I improve," she said dismally. "I *must* get more like his own people, and get on better with them, and all that. I *must*! Yet he doesn't tell me how to set to work; and it's hard to find out for oneself. I am trying; but it's very hard. If only somebody

E.W. HORNUNG

would show me how! For, unless I find out, he can't care about me much longer—I see it—he can't!"

Yet it seemed that he did.

If attending to the most extravagant wish most lightly spoken counts for anything, Alfred could certainly care for his wife still, and did care for her very dearly indeed. And that wish that Gladys had expressed while walking through the village of Ham—the desire to drive about in a coach-and-four—had been at least lightly uttered, and had never since crossed her mind, very possibly. Nevertheless, one day in the second week of June the coach-and-four turned up—spick and span, and startling and fairylike as Cinderella's famous vehicle. It was Alfred's surprise; he had got the coach for the rest of the season; and when he saw that his wife could find no words to thank him—but could only gaze at him in silence, with her lovely eyes grown soft and melting, and his hand pressed in hers—then, most likely, the honest fellow experienced a purer joy than he had ever known in all his life before. Nor did the surprise end there. By collusion with Lady Bligh and Granville, a strong party had been secretly convened for Ascot the very next day; and a charming dress, which Gladys had never ordered, came down from her dressmaker in Conduit Street that evening—when Alfred confessed, and was hugged. And thus, just as she was getting low and miserable and self-conscious, Gladys was carried off her feet and whirled without warning into a state of immense excitement.

Perhaps she could not have expressed her gratitude more eloquently than she did but a minute before they all drove off in the glorious June morning; when, getting her husband to herself for one moment, she flung her arms about his neck and whispered tenderly:—

"I'm going to be as good as gold all day—it's the least I can do, darling!"

And she was no worse than her word. The racing interested her vastly—she won a couple of sweepstakes too, by the way—yet all day she curbed her wild excitement with complete success. Only her dark eyes sparkled so that people declared they had never seen a woman so handsome, and in appearance so animated, who proved to have so little—so appallingly little—to say for herself. And it was Gladys herself who drove them all home again, handling the ribbons as no other woman handled them that season, and cracking her whip as very few men could crack one, so that it was heard for half a mile through the clear evening air, while for half that distance people twisted their necks and strained their eyes to see the last of the dark, bewitching, dashing driver who threaded her way with such nerve and skill through the moving maze of wheels and horseflesh that choked the country roads.

And, with it all, she kept her promise to the letter. And her husband was no less delighted than proud. And only her brother-in-law felt aggrieved.

"But it's too good to last," was that young man's constant consolation. "It's a record, so far; but she'll break out before the day is over; she'll entertain us yet—or I'll know the reason why!" he may have added in his most secret soul. At all events, as he sat next her at dinner, when the Lady Lettice Dunlop—his right-hand neighbour—remarked in a whisper the Bride's silence, Granville was particularly prompt to whisper back:—

"Try her about Australia. Sound her on the comparative merits of their races out there and Ascot. Talk in front of me, if you like; I don't mind; and she'll like it."

So Lady Lettice Dunlop leant over gracefully, and said she had heard of a race called the Melbourne Cup; and how did it compare with the Gold Cup at Ascot?

The Bride shook her head conclusively, and a quick light came into her eyes. "There is *no* comparison."

"You mean, of course, that your race does not compare with ours? Well, it hardly would, you know!" Lady Lettice smiled compassionately.

"Not a bit of it!" was the brusque and astonishing retort. "I mean that the Melbourne Cup knocks spots—I mean to say, is ten thousand times better than what we saw to-day!"

The Lady Lettice sat upright again and manipulated her fan. And it was Granville's opening.

"I can quite believe it," chimed in Gran. "I always *did* hear that that race of yours was the race of the world. Englishmen say so who have been out there, Lady Lettice. But you should tell us wherein the superiority lies, Gladys."

The Bride complied with alacrity.

"Why, the course is ever so much nicer; there are ever so many more people, but ever so much less crowding; the management of everything is ever so much better; and the dresses are gayer—*ever* so much!"

"Ever so much" was a recent reform suggested by Alfred. It was an undoubted improvement upon "a jolly sight," which it replaced; but, like most reforms, it was apt to be too much *en evidence* just at first.

She rattled off the points at a reckless rate, and paused fairly breathless. Her speaking looks and silent tongue no longer presented their curious contradiction; she not only looked excited, but spoke excitedly now. Lady Lettice smiled faintly, with elevated eyes and eyebrows, as she listened—till the comparison between Colonial and English dress, at which home-touch Lady Lettice was momentarily overcome behind her fan. But the Bride had other hearers besides Lady Lettice; and those who heard listened for more; and those who listened for more heard Granville remark pleasantly:—

"You used to come down from the Bush for the Melbourne Cup, then?"

"Did once," Gladys was heard to reply.

"Have a good time?"

"Did *so*."

"Old gentleman in luck, then?"

"Pretty well. No; not altogether, I think."

"Didn't care about going again, eh?"

"No; but that was because he knocked up when we got back."

The conversation had become entirely confidential between the two. Lady Lettice was out of it, and looked as though she were glad of that, though in reality she was listening with quite a fierce interest. Others were listening too, and not a few were watching the Bride with a thorough fascination: the good humour and high spirits with which she was now brimming over enhanced her beauty to a remarkable degree.

"What was it that knocked him up?" inquired Granville softly, but in distinct tones.

She smiled at him. "Never you mind!"

"But I am interested." He looked it.

She smiled at him again, not dreaming that any other eye was upon her; then she raised her champagne glass two inches from the table and set it down again; and her smile broadened, as though it were the best joke in the world.

The refined tale was told. The action was understood by all who had listened to what went before.

The Judge was one of those who both saw and heard; and he spoke to Granville on the subject afterwards, and with some severity. But Gran's defence was convincing enough.

"Upon my honour, sir," he protested, "I had no kind of idea what was coming."

"Well," said the Judge, grimly, "I hope *everybody* did not take it in. Her own father, too! Apart from the offensiveness of the revelation, there was a filial disrespect in it which, to me, was the worst part of it all."

Granville looked at his father humorously through his eyeglass.

"I fear, sir, she is like *our* noble Profession—no Respecter of Persons!"

But the Judge saw nothing to smile at. "It is nothing to joke about, my boy," he observed. "It has provoked me more than I can say. It is enough to frighten one out of asking people to the house. It forces me to do what I am very unwilling to do: I shall speak seriously to Alfred before we go to bed."

IX

E Tenebris Lux

Wild weather set in after Ascot. The break-up was sudden; in England it generally is. In a single night the wind flew into the east, and clouds swept into the sky, and thermometers and barometers went down with a run together. One went to bed on a warm, still, oppressive night in June; one got up four months later, in the rough October weather. The Bride came down shivering and aggrieved; the whims and frailties of the English climate were new to her, and sufficiently disagreeable. She happened to be down before any one else, moreover; and there were no fires in the rooms, which were filled with a cheerless, pallid light; while outside the prospect was dismal indeed.

The rain beat violently upon the windows facing the river, and the blurred panes distorted a picture that was already melancholy enough. The sodden leaves, darkened and discoloured by the rain, swung heavily and nervelessly in the wind; the strip of river behind the trees was leaden, like the sky, and separable from it only by the narrow, formless smear that marked the Surrey shore. In the garden, the paths were flanked with yellow, turbid runnels; the lawn alone looked happy and healthy; the life seemed drowned out of everything else—in this single night after Ascot. Gladys shivered afresh, and turned her back on the windows in miserable spirits. And, indeed, in downright depressing spectacles, a hopeless summer's day in the Thames Valley is exceptionally rich.

The Bride, however, had no monopoly of bad spirits that morning. This became plain at breakfast, but it was not so plain that the dejection of the others arose from the same simple cause as her own. Vaguely, she felt that it did not. At once she asked herself if aught that she had done or said unwittingly could be connected in any way with the general silence and queer looks; and then she questioned herself closely on every incident of the previous day and her own conduct therein—a style of self-examination to which Gladys was becoming sadly used. But no, she could remember nothing that she had done or said amiss yesterday. With respect to that day, at least, her conscience was clear. She could say the same of no other day, perhaps; but yesterday morning she had promised her husband golden behaviour; and she honestly believed, this morning, that she had kept her promise well. Yet *his* manner was strangest of all this morning, and particularly strange towards her, his wife. It was as though he had heard something against her. He barely looked at her. He only spoke to her to tell her that he must go up to town on business, and therefore alone; and he left without any tenderness in bidding her good-bye, though it was the first time he had gone up without her.

Gladys was distressed and apprehensive. What had she done? She did not know; nor could she guess. But she did know that the longer she stood in the empty rooms, and drummed with her fingers upon the cold, bleared panes, gazing out at the wretched day, the more she yearned for one little glimpse of the sunlit bush. The barest sand-hill on her father's run would have satisfied her so long as its contour came with a sharp edge against the glorious dark-blue sky; the worst bit of mallee scrub in all Riverina—with the fierce sun gilding the leaves—would have presented a more cheery prospect than this one on the banks of the renowned (but overrated) Thames. So thought Gladys; and her morning passed without aim or occupation, but with many sad reflections and bewildering conjectures, and in complete solitude; for Lady Bligh was upstairs in her little room, and everybody else was in town. Nor did luncheon enliven matters in the least. It was virtually a silent, as it was certainly a disagreeable, *tête-à-tête*.

And yet, though Lady Bligh went up again to her little room without so much as inquiring into her daughter-in-law's plans for the afternoon, neither was she without a slight twinge of shame herself.

"But I could not help it!" Lady Bligh exclaimed to herself more than once—so often, in fact, as to prove conclusively that she *could* have helped it. "I could not help it—indeed I could not. Once or twice I did try to say something—but there, I could not do it! After all, what have I to talk to her about? What is there in common between us? On the other hand, is not talking to her hanging oneself on tenter-hooks, for dread of what she will say next? And this is Alfred's wife! No pretensions—none of the instincts—no, not one!"

A comfortable fire was burning in the sanctum, lighting up the burnished brass of fender and guard and the brown tiles of the fireplace with a cheerful effect; and this made the chill gray light that hung over the writing-table under the window less inviting, if possible, than it had been before luncheon. Lady Bligh immediately felt that, for this afternoon, writing letters over there in the cold was out of the question.

She stood for a moment before the pleasant fire, gazing regretfully at Alfred's photograph on the chimney-piece. Then a thought smote her—heavily. She rang the bell. A maid answered it.

"Light a fire for Mrs. Alfred downstairs—in the morning-room, I think—and this minute. How dreadful of me not to think of it before!" said Lady Bligh, when the servant was gone. "Poor girl! Now I think of it, she *did* look cold at the table. I feel the cold myself to-day, but she must feel it ten times more, coming from that hot country. And I have had a fire all the morning, and she has not! She looked sad, too, as well as cold, now I think of it. I wonder why? She seems so unconscious of everything, so independent, so indifferent. And, certainly, I blame myself for seeing so little of her. But does the smallest advance ever come from *her* side? Does *she* ever try to meet *me* half-way? If only she had done so—if only she were to do so now—"

Lady Bligh stopped before following further a futile and mortifying train of speculation. No; it were better, after all, that no advances should be made now. It was a little too late for them. If, in the beginning, her daughter-in-law had come to her and sought her sympathy and her advice, it would have been possible then to influence and to help her; it might have been not difficult, even, to break to her—gently and with tact—many of her painful peculiarities as they appeared. But she had not come, and now it was too late. The account might have been settled item by item; but the sum was too heavy to deal with in the lump.

"Yet her face troubles me," said Lady Bligh. "It is so handsome, so striking, so full of character and of splendid possibilities; and I cannot understand why it should sometimes look so wistful and longing; for at all events this must be a very different—and surely a preferable—existence to her old rough life out there, with her terrible father" (Lady Bligh shuddered), "and no mother."

She could not write, so she drew the easy-chair close to the fire, and wrapped a shawl about her shoulders, and placed a footstool for her feet, and sat down in luxury with a Review. But neither could Lady Bligh read, and ultimately her brooding would probably have ended in a nap, had not some one tapped at the door.

Lady Bligh—a hater of indolence, who commonly practised her principle—being taken unawares, was weak enough to push back her chair somewhat, and to kick aside the footstool, before saying, "Come in." Then she looked round—and it was the Bride herself.

"Am I disturbing you very much?" asked Gladys, calmly; indeed, she shut the door behind her without waiting for the answer.

Lady Bligh was taken aback rather; but she did not show it. "Not at all. Pray come in. Is it something you want to ask me about?"

"There's lots of things I want to ask you about; if it isn't really bothering you too much altogether, Lady Bligh."

"Of course it is not, child; I should say so if it were," Lady Bligh answered, with some asperity. But her manner was not altogether discouraging.

"Thank you. Then I think I will sit down on that footstool by the fender—it is so cold. May I? Thanks. There, that won't keep the fire from you at all. Now, first of all, may I do *all* the questioning, Lady Bligh, please?"

Lady Bligh stared.

"What I mean is, may I ask you questions without you asking me any? You needn't answer if you don't like, you know. You may even get in a—in a rage with me, and order me out of the room, if you like. But please let me do the questioning."

"I am not likely to get in a rage with you," said Lady Bligh, dryly, "though I have no idea what is coming; so you had better begin, perhaps."

"Very well; then what I want to know is this—and I do want to know it very badly indeed. When you married, Lady Bligh, were you *beneath* Sir James?"

Lady Bligh sat bolt upright in her chair, and stared severely at her daughter-in-law. Gladys was sitting on the low stool with her hands clasped about her knees, and leaning backward with half her weight thus thrown upon her long straight arms. And she was gazing, not at the fire nor at Lady Bligh, but straight ahead at the wall in front of her. Her fine profile was stamped out sharply against the fire, yet touched at the edge with the glowing light, which produced a kind of Rembrandt effect. There was no movement of the long eyelashes projecting from the profile; the well-cut lips were firm. So far as could be seen from this silhouette, the Bride was in earnest. Lady Bligh checked the exclamation that had risen to her lips, and answered slowly:—

"I do not understand you, Gladys."

"No?" Gladys slowly turned her face to that of her companion; her eyes now seemed like still black pools in a place of shadows; and round her head the red firelight struggled through the loopholes and outworks of her hair. "Well, I mean—was it considered a very great match for *you?*"

"No; it certainly was not."

"Then he was not much above you—in riches or rank or anything else?"

"No; we were both very poor; our early days were a struggle."

"But you were equals from the very beginning—not only in money?"

"Yes; socially we were equals too."

Gladys turned her face to the fire, and kept it so turned. "I am rather sorry," she said at length, and sighed.

"You are sorry? Indeed!"

"Yes, Lady Bligh, and disappointed too; for I'd been hoping to find you'd been ever so much beneath Sir James. Don't you see, if you *had* been ever so much beneath him, you aren't a bit now; and it would have proved that the wife can become what the husband is, if she isn't that to begin with—and if she tries hard. No—you mustn't interrupt unless it's to send me away. I want you to suppose a case. Look back, and imagine that your own case was the opposite to what it really was. That Sir James was of a very good family. That you were not only not that, but were stupid and ignorant, and a worse thing—vulgar. That you had lived your rough life in another country; so that when he brought you to England as his wife, your head was full of nothing but that other country, which nobody wanted to know anything about. That you couldn't even talk like other people, but gave offence, not only without meaning to, but without knowing how. That—"

Lady Bligh could hear no more. "Oh, Gladys!" she exclaimed in a voice of pain, "you are not thinking of yourself?"

"That's a question! Still, as it's your first, I don't mind telling you you've hit it, Lady Bligh. I *am* thinking of myself. But you must let me finish. Suppose—to make short work of it—that you had been me, what would you have done to get different, like?"

"My poor child! I cannot bear to hear you talk like this!"

"Nonsense, Lady Bligh. I want you to tell me how you'd have gone about it—you know what I mean."

"I can't tell you, Gladys; I can't indeed!"

"What! Can't tell me what you would have done—what I ought to do?"

"I cannot!" Lady Bligh commanded her voice with difficulty. "I cannot!"

"Oh! then it's no good saying anything more about that." There was a touch of bitterness in the girl's tone. "But, at any rate, you might give me a hint or two how to be more like what you *are*. Can't you do that, even?"

"No, my dear—how can I? I am no model, Heaven knows!"

"Aren't you? Then I will get up. I am going, Lady Bligh. It's no good staying and bothering you any longer. I have asked my questions."

She rose sadly from the stool, and her eyes met Lady Bligh's again. For some minutes she had kept her face turned steadily to the fire. The rich warm glow of the fire still flushed her face and lingered in her luminous eyes. In the half-lit room, with the rain rattling ceaselessly against the panes, the presence of the Bride was especially attractive and comforting; but perhaps it was chiefly the rarity of her companionship to Lady Bligh that made the latter clutch Gladys's hand so eagerly.

"Don't go, my dear. Stop, and let us talk. This is practically our first talk together, Gladys, dear; you needn't be in such a hurry to end it. Sit down again. And—and I do wish you would not always call me 'Lady Bligh'!"

"Then what am I to call you, pray?" Gladys smiled up into the old lady's face; she could not help facing her now, for Lady Bligh would hold her hand; she was even forced to draw the footstool closer to the easy-chair; and thus she was now sitting at Lady Bligh's feet, touching her, and holding her hand.

"Could you not—sometimes—call me—'mother'?"

Gladys laughed. "It wouldn't be easy."

"But why not?"

"Because you could never be a mother to *me*. You might to another daughter-in-law, but not to me. You, who are so gentle and graceful and—and *everything*, could never seem like a mother to a—well, to me. People would say so, too, if they heard me call you 'mother.' It would make everybody laugh."

"Gladys! Gladys! How cruel you are to yourself! You are not what you say you are. Here—just now—"

"Ah," said the Bride, sadly. "Here! Just now! Yes, it is easy enough here and now. Here in the quiet, by the fireside, alone with you, it is easy enough to be well-behaved. I am on my good behaviour, and no one knows it better than I do. And I know it, too, when I behave badly; but not till afterwards. I go forgetting myself, you see. I believe it's principally when they talk to me about Australia. I suppose I lose my head, and talk wildly, and less like a lady than usual even. Alfred has told me, you see; though I don't know where it was I went wrong yesterday.

I thought I was so very good all day. I hardly opened my mouth to anybody. But somehow I can't help it when the Bush crops up. You see, I'm a Bush girl. *All* the girls out there aren't like me; don't you believe it. They would think me as bad as you do. I'm not a sample, you see. I should be riled if I was taken for one; nothing riles me so much as people speaking or thinking meanly of Australia! But here, alone with you, with everything so quiet, it would be difficult not to be quiet too. What's more, I like it, Lady Bligh—I do indeed. I can't come lady-like all at once, perhaps; but if I was oftener beside you, like just now, I might by degrees get more like you, Lady Bligh."

"Then you shall be oftener with me—you shall, my dear!"

"Thank you—thank you so much! And I shan't mind if you send me away; yet I won't speak if you're busy. If you'll only let me come in sometimes, for a little bit, that's all I ask."

"You shall come in as often as ever you like, my darling!"

The old lady had drawn her daughter-in-law's head backward upon her lap, and was caressing the lovely hair, more and more nervously, and bending over the upturned face. Gladys leant back with half-closed eyes. Suddenly a scalding drop fell upon her cheek. Next moment the girl was upon her feet. The moment after that she had fallen upon her knees and caught Lady Bligh's hands in her own.

"You are crying!" said Gladys, hoarsely. "You are crying, and because of me! Oh, Lady Bligh, forgive me! How could I know I should bring you such trouble as this? I never knew—I never dreamt it would be like this. Alfred told me that I should get on well with you all. He was blind, poor boy, but *I* might have known; only we loved each other so! Oh, forgive me—forgive me for marrying him! Say that you forgive me! Before God, I never thought it would be like this!"

"My daughter! I have nothing to forgive! Kiss me, Gladys—kiss me!"

"Yes, I will kiss you; but I have brought misery upon you all; and I will never forgive myself."

"Gladys—you have *not*! Do not think it—and don't go, Gladys."

"I must go. You have been good and kind to me; but this is hard for me too, though I am not crying. I never cry, though sometimes I feel inclined to, when I think of everything."

"But now you will often come beside me, Gladys?"

"Yes, I will come. And I will try to change; you have helped me already. It will not come all at once; but perhaps I can prevent myself giving you any fresh cause to be downright ashamed of me. Nay, I must. That's the least I can do. If I fail—"

She stopped, as though to think well of what she was saying. Her face became pale and stern—Lady Bligh never forgot it.

"If I fail," she repeated slowly, "after this, you will know that I am hopeless!"

She went to the door, but turned on the threshold, as though wishful to carry away a distinct impression of the scene—the half-lit room, the failing fire still reflected in the burnished brasses, the darkening panes still beaten by the wild rain, and the figure of Lady Bligh, dimly outlined and quivering with gentle weeping. Then she was gone.

X

Plain Sailing

Among unexpected pleasures there are few greater than the sudden discovery that one has become the living illustration of a common proverb. Of course the proverb must be of the encouraging order; but then most proverbs are. Equally of course, the conditions of this personal illustration should be exceptionally delightful; yet will there still remain an intrinsic charm in your relations with the proverb. You will feel benignantly disposed towards it for evermore. You will receive it henceforth with courtesy, even in the tritest application. Nor need the burden of obligation be all on your side: you can give that proverb a good character among your friends—a thing that few people will do for any proverb. You can tell it frankly: "Sir, I always thought you were a humbug, like the rest of them. Now I know better. I admit that I was hasty. I apologise. I shall speak up for *you*, sir, till my dying day!"

That good-hearted fellow, Alfred Bligh, awaking gradually to a sensation of this sort, became very rapidly the happiest of men. The proverb in his case was the one about the dawn and the darkest hour. Alfred's darkest hour had been the day after Ascot, when, after a perfectly amicable conversation with the Judge, he had rushed up to town with ice at his heart and schemes of instant removal in his head. His dawn was the same evening, at dinner, when an indefinable *je ne sais quoi* in the mutual manner of Gladys and his mother attracted his attention and held him in suspense. And after dinner his sun rose quickly up.

The happiness of the succeeding days—to Alfred, to Gladys, and to Lady Bligh—was complete and pure. Nothing much happened in those last perfect days of June, when the rain had all fallen, and the wind changed, and summer was come back. There was some rowing on the sunlit river, and a good deal of coaching, in small parties; but on the whole they were quiet days. Yet these were the days that stood out most plainly through the dim distance of after years.

To be closely intimate with Lady Bligh meant an intimacy with a nature that was generous and sweet and womanly; and it included a liberal education—for those who would help themselves to it—in gentle, unaffected manners. Gladys came under this very desirable influence at a favourable moment, and in precisely the right frame of mind to profit most by it. And profit she did. As she herself had predicted, no miracle was wrought; she did not become everything that she ought to have been in a day; but several small alterations of manner, all of them for the better, did very quickly take place.

The Bride felt her feet at last. Then, becoming thoroughly in touch with Lady Bligh, she waxed bold in a less approachable direction, and with the best results. Not only did she start lively little conversations with Sir James, but she got him to carry them on in the same light strain, and sustained her part in them very creditably indeed, all things considered. But the subject of his judicial functions was now avoided far more sedulously by Gladys than by the old gentleman himself. She even joined the Judge more than once in his early morning prowls; but the stock-whip was always left behind in her room. On these occasions she showed herself to be an admirable assistant-potterer; while she delighted her old companion still further by many pretty and even delicate attentions, to which he was not used, having no daughters of his own. Thus there were mornings when the Judge would come in to breakfast with quite a startling posy in his button-hole, and with a certain scarcely perceptible twitching of the lips and lowering of the eyelids, such as had been observed in him sometimes on the bench when the rest of the court were "convulsed with laughter." It invariably transpired that the decoration was the work and gift of the Judge's daughter-in-law; and, as the old gentleman had never before been seen by his family to sport any such ornament, the departure was extremely gratifying to most of them.

Granville, it is true, found fault with the taste displayed in the composition of the button-holes, and one morning flatly refused one that had been made for him expressly; but the fact is, Granville was of rather small account in the house just now. He was busy, certainly, and was seen very little down at Twickenham; but he might have been seen more—his temporary occupation of a back-seat was in a great measure voluntary. Nor was he really malicious at this time. It is true that he spoke of the leopard's spots, and used other phrases equally ominous but less hackneyed; for the most part, however, he made these observations to himself. He could have found nowhere a more appreciative and sympathetic audience. But, though he looked on sardonically enough at the Bride's conquests, Granville did not lay himself out to hinder them. This should be clearly understood. The fellow was not a full-blown Mephistopheles.

And the happy pair were indeed happy. But for an occasional wistful, far-away look—such as will come sometimes to every exile, for all the "pleasures and palaces" of new worlds—Gladys seemed to everybody to be gay and contented as the midsummer days were long. As for Alfred, he considered the sum of his earthly happiness complete. Even the ideal farm (which his solicitors were doing their best to find for him) in the ideal sleepy hollow (which *he* meant to do *his* best to wake up, by the introduction of vigorous Bush methods)—when purchased, stocked, furnished, inhabited, and in full swing—could not, he felt, add much to his present happiness. Poor Alfred! He was laying out the future on idyllic lines. But, meanwhile, the present was full of happy days; and that was well.

There was one evening that Alfred did not soon forget.

It was the last Sunday in June. There had been a thunderstorm early in the afternoon and a smart shower. The evening air was a long, cool, delicious draught, flavoured with the exquisite fragrance of dripping leaves and petals; and this, and the sound of the church bells, and the sunlight glittering upon the wet lanes, came back to Alfred afterwards as often as he remembered the conversation which made the walk to the old church all too short. Alfred walked with his mother; Gladys, some little distance ahead, with the Judge.

"I think Gladys likes England a little better now," observed Lady Bligh.

"And can't England say the same thing of Gladys?" cried Alfred. "Don't answer the question—it's idiotic. But oh, mother, I'm a fool with very joy!"

"Because Gladys has won all our hearts, dear?"

"Yes; and I really think she has. You have all been so good, so patient and forgiving. Don't stop me, mother. If you had been different, I know I never should have allowed that you had anything to forgive; but now that you are like this, I own that there was much. Look at her now with the Judge; he has given her his arm. Now think of the beginning between these two!"

"Why think of that? We have all forgotten it. You must forget it too."

"I think of it," said Alfred, "because it is all over; because you have civilised my wild darling; and because I like to realise this. But, upon my soul, if you had seen her life out there; if you knew her father (she doesn't remember her mother); if you had any idea of the work she did on that run; you would simply be amazed—as I am, now that I look back upon it—at what your tenderness has done. But do you know, mother, what the dear girl says? I had nearly forgotten to tell you."

One would have counted upon a joke, and possibly a good one; for Alfred stopped to chuckle before coming out with it; though, certainly Alfred was not the best judge of jokes.

"She says that if ever she makes you feel regularly ashamed of her again, she may be considered hopeless; and though you forgive her, she'll never forgive herself! That's rather rich, eh?"

Lady Bligh failed to see it in that light. On the contrary, for one moment she seemed both surprised and pained.

"Perhaps, Alfred," she said, thoughtfully, "she still feels the restraint, and hates our conventionalities. I often think she must; I sometimes think she does."

"Not she! Not a bit of it! She's as safe as the Bank, and as happy as they make 'em, I know her!"

Poor Alfred!

"Perhaps," said Lady Bligh again; "but there may be a constant effort which we cannot see; and I have once or twice caught a look in her eyes—but let that pass. I may be wrong; only I think it has been rather slow for her lately. She must have more amusement. There are one or two amusing things coming on presently. But just now I should like to think of something quite fresh to interest her. My dear boy! you are whistling!—in the churchyard!"

In fact, Alfred was foolish with joy, as he himself had said. He could not control his spirits long when speaking of Gladys, and hearing her well spoken of by the others, and marvelling at the change that a few days had brought about. It was a case of either laughing or crying with him then; and the tears never got a chance.

But, in the solemn twilight of the church; standing, kneeling, sitting by his wife's side; sharing her book; listening with her to the consummate language of the Common Prayer; watching with her the round stained window fail and fade against the eastern sky—then, indeed, the boisterous, boyish spirits of this singularly simple-minded man of thirty melted into thankfulness ineffable and perfect peace.

It so happened that they sang an anthem in the old church that evening. This neither attracted nor distracted Alfred at first. He was a man without very much more music in his soul than what he was able to whistle when in high spirits. It did not strike him that this anthem was lovelier than most "tunes." The sweet sensations that stole over his spirit as the singing of it proceeded certainly were not credited to the music. To the words he never would have attempted to listen but for an accident.

To Alfred the anthem presented but one of the many opportunities presented by the Church Service for private reverie on the part of worshippers. Of course his reverie was all about the future and Gladys. And while he mused his arm touched hers, that was the delightful part of it. But on glancing down to see her face again (he had actually not looked upon it for five whole minutes) his musing swiftly ended. Her singular expression arrested his whole attention. And this was the accident that made him listen to the words of the anthem, to see if *they* could have affected her so strangely.

The Bride's expression was one of powerful yearning. The first sentence Alfred managed to pick out from the words of the anthem was: "Oh, for the wings, for the wings of a dove!" piped in a boy's high treble.

The melting wistfulness in the Bride's liquid eyes seemed to penetrate through that darkening east window into far-away worlds; and the choir-boy sang: "Far away, far away would I rove!"

The solo went on:

> *In the wilderness build me a nest:*
> *And remain there for ever at rest.*

Then, with some repetition which seemed vain to Alfred, the chorus swallowed the solo. And to Alfred's mind the longing in his wife's face had grown definite, acute, and almost terrible.

As they knelt down after the anthem, his eyes met those of his mother. She, too, had seen Gladys's expression. Was it the expression she had referred to on the way to church? Was such an expression a common one with his darling, and concealed only from him? Was it possible that she was secretly longing and pining for the Bush—now— when they were all so happy?

Much later in the evening—long after church—Lady Bligh made an opportunity of speaking again alone with Alfred. "I have been maturing my little plans," she said, smiling.

"As regards Gladys?" he asked.

"Yes; and I have been thinking that really, after all, she need not be so dull during the next few days—"

Alfred interrupted her hastily.

"I also have been thinking; and, do you know, after all, I half fancy that she *is* a bit dull. I shall be very glad indeed if you have thought of something to "liven her up a little."

Lady Bligh regarded him shrewdly; but she was not entirely astonished at this complete change of opinion. She, too, had seen Gladys's longing, far-away expression in church. She, too, remembered it.

"Well, she will be less dull during the next few days than just lately," said Lady Bligh, after a slight pause. "On Tuesday, to begin with, there is this garden-party of ours; a dull thing enough in itself, but the people may amuse Gladys. On Wednesday, there is to be the Opera for her, at last. Thursday and Friday you must boat and drive. But for Saturday— when the Lord Chief is coming—you are all invited to lawn-tennis somewhere; are you not? After this week it is simply *embarras*; the two matches at Lord's, and Henley too, one on top of the other; then Wimbledon. Gladys must miss none of these. But can you guess what my happy thought is?"

"You seem to have so many happy thoughts!"

"No; but my little plan for to-morrow?"

"I have no idea. But I think Gladys would be content to do nothing much to-morrow, perhaps."

"Alfred," said Lady Bligh, severely, "Gladys tells me you have never once had her in the Park! How is that?"

"I—well, the fact is, I'm such a duffer in the *very* swagger part of the town," said poor Alfred; "and I never did know the run of the parks properly."

"Then you shall drive with Gladys and me, and learn. It is getting near the end of the season, when every day makes a difference. So, not to lose another day, we'll drive in to-morrow. This is my happy thought! I think Gladys will like it—though Garrod won't."

"You mean he'll say it's too much for *his* horses? I should think he'll give warning," said Alfred, encouragingly.

"He may," said Lady Bligh, with a fine fearlessness which can be properly appraised only by ladies who keep, or once kept, their coachman. "He may. I defy him!"

XI

A Thunder-Clap

Fully ten days were wanting before the Eton and Harrow cricket-match, which appears to be pretty generally recognised as the last "turn" in the great variety entertainment of the season; there was plenty of life, and of high life, too, in the town yet; and, what was even more essential to a thorough enjoyment of the Park, the afternoon, as regarded the weather, was for once beyond all praise. Moreover, Royalty was there for at least half an hour; so that the circumstances attendant upon young Mrs. Bligh's first appearance in the ring of fashion were in every way all that could be desired.

It was an "appearance"; for Lady Bligh, though in no sense a woman of fashion, was sufficiently well known to attract attention, which was heightened by the increasing rarity of her appearances in the fashionable world. Even had it been otherwise, the robust, striking beauty of the dark young woman at her side must have awakened interest on its own account. It did, among those who did not know the Blighs by sight. But with most people the questions were: Where had Lady Bligh discovered such a fresh and taking type of prettiness? Was the girl a relative? Was that Alfred Bligh sitting opposite to the ladies, come back from Australia disfigured by a beard? Was she his fiancée—or were they already married? It is intended by no means to imply that the modest and even homely equipage of Lady Bligh became the cynosure of Hyde Park; but it was certainly seen; and few saw it with unawakened curiosity.

One or two persons were able to satisfy to some extent this curiosity, and took a delight in doing so; Lady Lettice Dunlop, for one. The curiosity that Lady Lettice relieved was of a languid and peculiarly well-bred kind. A coronet adorned the barouche in which she rode. She said rather more than she knew, yet not quite all that she did know, and said it with a gentle disdain. But Lady Lettice was stopped by a deprecatory gesture of her mother the Countess before she came to the end—which made her regret having over-elaborated the beginning. The Countess considered the story most coarse, and regretted the almost friendly nature of the bow with which she had just favoured poor Lady Bligh. Yet, as the Lady Lettice was generous enough to fancy, the

Colonial creature did seem on her very best behaviour this afternoon. And in her fancy Lady Lettice was nearer the mark than in her facts.

Another person, in an even better position to answer questions concerning the Bride, was Mr. Travers, M.P.—now the newest M.P. but one. He was walking under the trees with his daughter, whom he was boring somewhat with his political "shop"; for he was enough of a new boy still to be full of his nice new lessons. This Miss Travers, however, was no young girl, but a woman of thirty, with a kind, sweet, sympathetic face, and a nature intensely independent. She was best known for her splendid work in Whitechapel, though how splendid that work really was no one knew outside the slums, where her face was her only protection—but a greater one than a cordon of police. But she had also a reputation as a singer, which need not have been confined to a few drawing-rooms in the West, and numberless squalid halls in the East, had she been ambitiously inclined. And this Miss Travers was attracted and charmed by the bold, conspicuous beauty of young Mrs. Bligh; pressed for an introduction; pressed all the harder on hearing some plain truths about the Bride and her Bush manners; and presently had her way.

It was now six o'clock. The crowning period of the afternoon had commenced with the arrival of Royalty a few minutes before the hour. Carriages were drawn up by the rails on either side in long, regular ranks. The trough between presented visions of glossy horseflesh and flashing accoutrements and flawless japan, to say nothing of fine looks and finer dress; visions changeful as those of the shaken kaleidoscope; marvellous, magical visions—no matter how much or how little they owed to the golden glamour of the sinking sun, visions of intrinsic wonder.

The Blighs' serviceable vehicle had found an anchorage by the inner rails in the thick of all this, but not in the thickest. They were, in fact, no farther than a furlong from the Corner, and thus in comparatively open water. At this point the shrubs planted between the two converging courses come to an end, and the two roads are separated by little more than twenty yards. A little way farther on you can see only the bobbing heads of the riders over in Rotten Row; but at this point you have indeed "the whole show" before you. The position had been taken up on the Bride's express petition. It was the riding that interested Gladys. She had no eyes for the smart people in the carriages when once she could watch with as little trouble the hacks and their riders in Rotten Row. The little interest she took in the passing and re-passing of Royalty was somewhat disappointing. But it was plain that she was enjoying herself in her own way; and that was everything. When the Traverses came up, the interruption of this innocent enjoyment was a distinct annoyance to Gladys.

Alfred—to whom it was not an afternoon of wild delight—got out of the carriage with some alacrity; and Miss Travers, with a very engaging freedom of manner, got in. She button-holed the Bride (if that is not an exclusively masculine act—as between man and man), and at first the Bride did not like it. Very soon, however, Gladys was pleased to withdraw her attention, partially, from Rotten Row and transfer it to Miss Travers. Like everybody else, the Bride was immensely attracted; Miss Travers's manner was so sympathetic, yet unaffected, and so amazingly free (Gladys thought) from English stiffness; and her face was infinitely kind and sweet, and her voice musical and soft.

So Mr. Travers, with one foot upon the carriage-step, brought Lady Bligh up to date in her politics generally, and in his own political experiences in particular; and Alfred made aimless patterns on the ground with his feet; and Miss Travers questioned Gladys on the subject upon which all strangers who were told where she came from invariably and instantly did question her. But Miss Travers did this in a way of her own, and a charming way. You would have thought it had been the dream of her life to go to Australia; you would have inferred that it was her misfortune and not her fault that her lines were cast in England instead of out there; and yet you would not, you could not, have suspected her of hypocrisy. She was one of those singular people who seem actually to prefer, in common conversation, the *tuum* to the *meum*. Gladys was charmed. But still she stole furtive glances across the space dividing them from the tan; and her answers, which would have been eager and impetuous enough in any other circumstances, came often slowly; she was obviously *distraite*.

Miss Travers saw this, and followed the direction of the dark, eager eyes, and thought she understood. But suddenly there came a quick gleam into the Bride's eyes which Miss Travers did not understand. A horsewoman was crossing their span of vision in the Row at a brisk canter. The Bride became strangely agitated. Her face was transfigured with surprise and delight and incredulity. Her lips came apart, but no breath escaped them. Her flashing eyes followed the cantering horsewoman, who, in figure and in colouring, if not in feature, was just such another as Gladys herself, and who sat her horse to perfection.

But she was cantering past; she would not turn her head, she would not look; a moment more and the shrubs would hide her from Gladys—perhaps for ever.

Before that moment passed, Gladys stood up in the carriage, trembling with excitement. Careless of the place—forgetful of Lady Bligh, of all that had passed, of the good understanding so hardly gained—attracting the attention of Royalty by conspicuously turning her back upon them as they passed for the fourth time—the Bride encircled her lips with her two gloved palms, and uttered a cry that few of the few hundreds who heard it ever forgot:—

"*Coo-ee!*"

That was the startling cry as nearly as it can be written. But no letters can convey the sustained shrillness of the long, penetrating note represented by the first syllable, nor the weird, die-away wail of the second. It is the well-known Bush call, the "jodel" of the black-fellow; but it has seldom been heard from a white throat as Gladys Bligh let it out that afternoon in Hyde Park, in the presence of Royalty.

To say that there was a sensation in the vicinity of the Blighs' carriage—to say that its occupants were for the moment practically paralysed—is to understate matters, rather. But, before they could recover themselves, the Bride had jumped from the carriage, pressed through the posts, rushed across to the opposite railings, and seized in both hands the hand of the other dark and strapping young woman, who had reined in her horse at once upon the utterance of the "*Coo-ee!*"

And there was a nice little observation, audible to many, which Gladys had let fall in flying:—

"Good Lord deliver us—it's *her*!"

XII

Past Pardon

Patience and sweetness of disposition may not only be driven beyond endurance; they may be knocked outside in, knocked into their own antitheses. And one need not go to crime or even to sin to find offences which no amount of abstract angelicalness could readily forgive or ever forget. It is a sufficiently bad offence, if not an actual iniquity, to bring well-to-do people into public derision through an act of flagrant thoughtlessness and unparalleled social barbarity. But if the people are not only well-to-do, but well and honourably known, and relatives by your marriage, who have been more than kind to you, you could scarcely expect a facile pardon. Sincerity apart, they would be more than mortal if they so much as pretended to forgive you out of hand, and little less than divine if they did not tell you at once what they thought of you, and thereafter ignore you until time healed their wounds.

Woman of infinite sweetness though she was, Lady Bligh was mortal, not divine; and she showed her clay by speaking very plainly indeed, as the carriage swept out of the Park, and by speaking no more (to Gladys) that day. A good deal of cant is current about people whose anger is violent ("while it lasts"), but short-lived ("he gets over it in a moment"); but it is difficult to believe in those people. If there be just cause for wrath, with or without violence, it is not in reason that you can be in a rollicking good humour the next minute. That is theatrical anger, the anger of the heavy father. Lady Bligh, with all her virtues, could nurse the genuine passion—an infant that thrives at the breast. Indeed, it is probable that before the end of the silent drive to Twickenham (Alfred never opened his clenched teeth all the way) this thoroughly good woman positively detested the daughter whom she had just learnt to love. For it is a fallacy to suppose that the pepper-and-salt emotion of love and hatred in equal parts is the prerogative of lovers; you will find it oftener in the family.

What penitence Gladys had expressed had been lame—crippled by an excuse. Moreover, her tone had lacked complete contrition. Indeed, if not actually defiant, her manner was at least repellent. She had been spoken to hotly; some of the heat was reflected; it was a hot moment.

As for her excuse, it, of course, was ridiculous—*qua* excuse.

She had seen her oldest—indeed, her only—girl friend, Ada Barrington. Ada (Gladys pronounced it "Ida") was another squatter's daughter; their fathers had been neighbours, more or less, for many years; but Ada's father owned more stations than one, was a wealthy man—in fact, a "woollen king." Gladys had known they were in Europe, but that was all. And she had seen Ada cantering past, but Ada had not seen her. So she had "*coo-ee'd*." What else was there to be done? Gladys did not exactly ask this question, but she implied it plainly. As it happened, if she had not "*coo-ee'd*," she never would have seen Ada again, to a certainty; for the Barringtons had taken a place in Suffolk, and were going down there the very next day. That was all. Perhaps it was too much.

Silence ensued, and outlasted the long drive. What afterwards passed between the young husband and wife did not, of course, transpire. There was no further expression of regret than the very equivocal and diluted apology comprehended in the Bride's excuses; indeed, Lady Bligh and her daughter-in-law never spoke that night; nor did Alfred attempt to mediate between them. As a matter of fact, his wife had told him—with a recklessness that cut him to the heart—that, this time, she neither expected nor deserved, nor so much as desired, any one's forgiveness; that now she knew what she had feared before, that she was hopeless; that—but the rest was wild talk.

Next morning, however, Alfred went to Lady Bligh with a letter, one that Gladys had received by the early post. It was an invitation from the Barringtons, the wording of which was sufficiently impulsive and ill-considered. Ada besought her darling Gladys to go stay with them in Suffolk immediately, on the following Saturday, and for as many days as she could and would; and the invitation included the darling's husband in a postscript.

"An extraordinary kind of invitation!" observed Lady Bligh, handing back the letter.

"Ignorance," said Alfred laconically.

"Did you meet the people out there?"

"Only this girl's brother; the others had been in Europe some time. I thought him a very pleasant fellow, I remember, though his contempt for me and for all 'home' birds was magnificent."

"Well," said Lady Bligh, "it is hardly the kind of invitation that Gladys can accept. Is it?"

"She refuses to think of it," Alfred answered, with a frown that rather puzzled Lady Bligh. "But I hope she will change her mind. I wish her to go."

His mother was silent for more than a minute. "Does the letter say Saturday?" she then inquired.

"Yes." Alfred gazed steadily in his mother's face as though he would search her inmost thoughts. "Yes, it says Saturday. And it is on Saturday that the Lord Chief is coming down to stay over Sunday, is it not? I thought so. I very much wish I could induce her to go."

"Not on that account, my boy, I hope?" Lady Bligh seemed slightly embarrassed.

"Partly," said Alfred, speaking firmly and distinctly, but not without an effort; "partly on that account, but by no means altogether."

"She could not go without you," remarked Lady Bligh; "and they do not ask you civilly, to say the least of it."

"She *could* go without me," returned Alfred emphatically. "What's more, I want her to. It's she that won't hear of it. These are quite old and intimate friends of Gladys and her father. She might easily spend a week with them alone, without me. Mother—I think she would like it so, if only she would go! They are probably free-and-easy, roughish folks, and it would do her good, a week with them. There would be no restraints—nay, she has observed none here, God knows!—but there there might be none to observe. She could do and say what she liked. She would hurt no one's feelings. She would scandalise no one. And— do you know what, mother?—I have got it into my head that when she came back she would see the difference, and appreciate your ways here more than she ever might otherwise. I have got it into my head that one week of that kind, just now, would open her eyes for good and all. And I think—there might be no more relapses! Yes, I thought that before; but I was wrong, you see—after yesterday! Besides, this week would bring us within a few weeks of Scotland; and, after Scotland, we shall have our own little place to go to—I have almost settled upon one. But if I went with her, restraint would go with her too."

His voice had broken more than once with emotion. He commanded it with difficulty, and it became hard and unnatural. In this tone he added:—

"Besides—it would be more comfortable for every one if she were not here with the Lord Chief Justice."

"Do not say that—do not think that!" said Lady Bligh; but faintly, because her heart echoed his sentiment.

"Oh, there's no disguising it—my wife's dynamite!" said Alfred, with a short, harsh laugh. "Only an explosion is worse at one time than at another." He went hastily from the room, neither of them having referred more directly to the scandalous scene in the Park.

He went straight to his wife, to try once more to coax her into accepting the Barringtons' invitation. But it was of no use. She would not listen to him. She would go nowhere without her husband; she should write that to Ada plainly.

Later in the morning, Lady Bligh, of her own deliberate design, came in contact with her daughter-in-law. Gladys attempted escape. Lady Bligh caught her by the hand.

"You are angry, Gladys!"

Gladys said nothing.

"I don't think *you* are the one to be angry," Lady Bligh said, nettled by the other's sullen manner.

Gladys raised her eyes swiftly from the ground; they were filled with bitterness. "Haven't I a right to be what I like with myself?" she cried. "I am angry with no one else. But I shall never forgive myself—no, nor I won't be forgiven either; I am hopeless! I feared it before; now I know it. Let me go, Lady Bligh!"

She broke away, and found a quiet spot, by-and-by, among the trees by the river.

"If only I were in *there*!" cried Gladys, out of the tumult of shame and rebellion within her. "In there—or else back in the Bush! And one is possible and easy; and the other is neither!"

By a single grotesque act she had brought her happiness, and not hers alone, to wreck and ruin!

XIII

A Social Infliction

Happily for all concerned, there was something else to be thought about that day: it was the day of Lady Bligh's garden-party.

The British garden-party is possibly unique among the social gatherings of the world. It might be a revelation to most intelligent foreigners. It is held, of course, in the fresh air; the weather, very likely, is all that can be desired. The lawn is soft and smooth and perfectly shaven; sweeping shadows fall athwart it from the fine old trees. The flower-beds are splendidly equipped; their blended odours hover in the air. The leaves whisper and the birds sing. The scene is agreeably English. But let in the actors. They are English too. The hostess on the lawn receiving the people, and slipping them through her busy fingers into solitude and desolation—anywhere, anywhere, out of her way; the stout people in the flimsy chairs, in horrid jeopardy which they alone do not realise; the burly, miserable male supers, in frock-coats and silk hats, standing at ease (but only in a technical sense) around the path, ashamed to eat the ices that the footman proffers them, ashamed of having nobody to talk to but their sisters or wives—who are worse than no one: it is so feeble to be seen speaking only to *them*. This is the British garden-party in the small garden, in the suburbs. In the large garden, in the country, you may lose yourself among the fruit-trees without being either missed or observed; but this is not a point in favour of the institution. Even in suburban districts there are bold spirits that aspire to make their garden-parties different from everybody else's, and not dull; who write "Lawn Tennis" in the corner of their invitation-cards before ascertaining the respective measurements of a regulation court and of their own back gardens. But beware of these ambitious souls; they add yet another terror to the British garden-party. To go in flannels and find everybody else in broadcloth; to be received as a champion player in consequence, and asked whether you have "entered at Wimbledon"; to be made to play in every set (because you are the only man in flannels), with terrible partners, against adversaries more terrible still—with the toes of the onlookers on the side lines of the court, and the dining-room windows in peril should you but swing back your racket for your usual smashing service, once in a way, to show them how it is done: all this amounts to spending your afternoon in purgatory, in the section reserved for impious lawn-tennis players. Yet nothing is more common. The lawn must be utilised, either for lawn-tennis or for bowls (played with curates), or by the erection of a tent for refreshments. By Granville's intervention, the Blighs had the refreshment-tent.

Lady Bligh would not have given garden-parties at all, could she have been "at home" in any other way; but as her set was largely composed of people living actually in town, who would not readily come ten miles out for a dinner-party, still less for an after-dinner party, she had really no choice in the matter. Still, Lady Bligh's garden-parties were not such very dull affairs after all. They were immensely above the suburban average. To the young and the curious they held out attractions infinitely greater than garden-party lawn-tennis, though these could not be advertised on the cards of invitation. For instance, you were sure of seeing a celebrity or two, if not even the highest dignitaries, with some of the dignity in their pockets. And it is inexpressible how delightful it was to come across a group of Her Majesty's Judges gorging strawberry ices unblushingly in a quiet corner of the marquee. On the present occasion, when the stoutest and most pompous Q.C. at the Bar—Mr. Merivale—sat down on the slenderest chair in the garden, and thence, suddenly, upon the grass, the situation was full of charm for Granville and some of his friends, who vied with one another in a right and proper eagerness to help the great man to his feet. Even Gladys (who was so very far from being in a laughing mood) laughed at this; though she was not aware that the stout gentleman was a Q.C., nor of the significance of those initials, had any one told her so.

But this was all the entertainment that Gladys extracted from the long afternoon. She was amused, at the moment, in spite of herself; she was not amused a second time. She kept ingeniously in the background. Alfred was attentive to her, of course, but not foolishly attentive, this afternoon. And Granville introduced to her one of his clean-shaven friends, whom Gladys conversed with for perhaps a minute. She was also presented by the Judge—in his recent genial, fatherly manner—to one or two of his colleagues. Plainly, the disgraceful scene in Hyde Park had not yet reached Sir James's ears. But that scandal was being discreetly discussed by not a few of the guests. Gladys suspected as much, though she did not know it. She imagined herself to be a not unlikely subject of conversation in any case, but quite a tempting one in the light of her last escapade. But this idea did not worry her. In some moods it is possible to be acutely self-conscious without being the least sensitive; Gladys's present mood was one. More often than at the people, she gazed at the window of her own room, and longed to be up there, alone. She neither took any interest in what was going on around her, nor cared what the people were whispering concerning her. No doubt they *were* whispering, but what did it matter? Misery is impervious to scorn and ridicule and contempt. These things wound the vanity; misery deadens it. Gladys was miserable.

Among the later arrivals was Miss Travers. Her father could not come: he was doing the fair thing by the Party and his constituents: it was his first term. Miss Travers came alone, and intended to go back alone, the later the better. Whitechapel had made her fearless and independent. She rather hoped to be asked to stop to dinner: some people were certain to stay, for the Blighs were uncommonly hospitable, and in many things quite unconventional; and Miss Travers intended to be one of those people, if she got the opportunity. She also intended to cultivate the most original specimen of her sex that she had ever yet met with; and for this she tried to make the opportunity.

But the most original of her sex was also one of the most slippery, when she liked; she dodged Miss Travers most cleverly, until the pursuer was herself pursued, and captured. Her captor was a rising solicitor, a desirable gentleman and an open admirer; but he did not improve his chances by that interview. Miss Travers was disappointed, almost annoyed. The unlucky lawyer sought to make her smile with a story: the story of the "*coo-ee!*" as he had heard it. He knew Miss Travers intimately; her appreciation of humour was vast, for a woman; he felt sure she would be tickled. But, unfortunately, the version he had heard was already fearfully exaggerated, and, as Miss Travers drew him on gently, yet without smiling as he wished her to, the good fellow improvised circumstances still more aggravating and scandalous; and then—sweet Miss Travers annihilated him in a breath.

"I was in their carriage at the time, myself; but—you will excuse my saying so—I shouldn't have recognised the incident from your description!"

It was a staggerer; but Miss Travers did not follow up the blow. She reproved him, it is true, but so kindly, and with such evident solicitude for his moral state, that the wretch was in ecstasies in two minutes.

"At all events," he said, with enthusiasm, "she has you for her champion! I won't hear another word about her; *I'll* champion her too!"

"If you spoke to her for one moment," Miss Travers replied, "you would own yourself that she is charming. You never saw such eyes!"

This the lawyer seemed to question, by the rapt manner in which he gazed into Miss Travers's own eyes; but the speech was the prettier for being left unspoken; and here the lawyer showed some self-restraint and more wisdom. But immediately the lady left him: she had descried her quarry.

Gladys dodged again, and, passing quickly through the tent, heard two words that sent the blood to her cheeks. The words were in close conjunction—"*coo-ee!*" and "disgrace." Without turning to see who had uttered them—the voice was unfamiliar—she hurried through into the house, and finding the little morning-room quite empty, went in there to sit down and think.

She was not wounded by the chance words; her lifeless pride had not quickened and become vulnerable all in a moment—it was not that. But it was this: what she had done, she realised now, for the first time, fully. Disgrace! She had disgraced Lady Bligh, Sir James, Alfred, Granville, all of them; in a public place, she, the interloper in the family, had brought down disgrace upon them all. Disgrace!—that was what people were saying. Disgrace to the Blighs—that was why she minded what the people said. And she minded this so much, now, that she rocked herself to and fro where she sat, and wrung her large strong hands, and groaned aloud.

And it was not only once; she had disgraced them many times. And all had been forgiven. But this could never be forgiven.

If only she had never married poor Alfred; if only she had never come among his family, to behave worse than their very servants! The servants? Would Bella Bunn have behaved so in her place? It was not likely, for even Bella had been able to give her hints, and she had consulted Bella upon points on which she would have been ashamed to confess her ignorance, even to Alfred. But, in spite of all their goodness and patience, she had brought only unhappiness to them all; there could be no more happiness for them or for her while she remained in the family.

"I ought to be dead—or back in the Bush!" she cried again, in her heart. "Oh, if only one was as easy as the other!"

These were her sole longings. Of the two, one was strong and not new

E.W. HORNUNG

(being intensified, not produced, by the circumstances), but sufficiently impracticable. The other was easy to compass, easy to the point of temptation, but as yet not nearly so strong, being entirely the impulse of events. But neither longing was at present anything more than a longing; no purpose showed through either yet. The reality of Alfred's love, the feeling that it would kill him to lose her, was accountable for this. Gladys's resolution was, so far, a blank tablet, not because purpose was absent, but because it was not yet become visible.

A rough analogy may be borrowed from the sensitive film used for the production of a photographic negative. The impression is taken, yet the film remains blank as it was before, until the proper acid is applied, when the impression becomes visible.

Now, a moral acid, acting upon that blank tablet of the mind, would produce a precisely similar effect. Suppose Gladys became convinced that Alfred would be a happier man without her, that it would be even a relief to him to lose her: this would supply the moral acid.

The effect of this moral acid would coincide with that of the photographer's acid. In either case something that had been imperceptible hitherto would now start out in sharp outline. The blank film would yield the negative picture; the vague longings of Gladys would take the shape of two distinct alternatives, one of them inevitable.

Suppose this happened, one of these alternatives was so simple as to be already, in its embryo state, something of a temptation; while the other would remain a moral impossibility.

It must be remembered that the Bride confronted no such alternatives yet, but merely experienced vague, passionate longings. In this state of mind, however, but one drop of acid was needed to produce "development."

XIV

"Hear My Prayer!"

Miss Travers did not, after all, succeed in cornering Gladys at the garden-party, but she did contrive to get herself asked to stay later, and without much difficulty (she would probably have found it far more difficult to go with the rest—hostesses were tenacious of Miss Travers); and after dinner, when the ladies went off to the drawing-room, her stubborn waiting was at last rewarded.

Some other people had stayed to dinner also, in the same informal way, and among them one or two of Granville's friends. These young men had come to the garden-party by no advice of Gran's—in fact, those who chanced to have mentioned to him Lady Bligh's invitation he had frankly told to stay away and not to be fools. But, having come, he insisted on their staying. "For," he said, "you deserve compensation, you fellows; and the Judge's wine, though I say it, hasn't a fault—unless it's spoiling a man for his club's."

And while the young men put the truth of this statement to a more earnest test than could be applied before the ladies left the table, Miss Travers, in the drawing-room, at last had Gladys to herself. And Miss Travers was sadly disappointed—as, perhaps, she deserved to be. Gladys had very little to say to her. As a matter of fact, it was no less irksome to the Bride to listen than to talk herself. But they happened to be sitting close to the piano, and it was not long before a very happy thought struck Gladys, which she instantly expressed in the abrupt question:—

"You sing, Miss Travers, don't you?"

"In a way."

"In a way! I've heard all about the way!" Gladys smiled; Miss Travers thought the smile sadly changed since yesterday. "Sing now."

"You really want me to?"

"Yes, really. And you must." Gladys opened the piano.

Miss Travers sang a little song that Gladys had never heard before, accompanying herself from memory. She sang very sweetly, very simply—in a word, uncommonly well. The voice, to begin with, was an exceptionally sound soprano, but the secret and charm of it all was,

E.W. HORNUNG

of course, in the way she used her voice. Gladys had asked for a song to escape from a chat, but she had forgotten her motive in asking—she had forgotten that she *had* asked for it—she had forgotten much that it had seemed impossible to forget, even thus, for one moment—before the song was half finished. Very possibly, with Gladys, who knew nothing of music, this was an appeal to the senses only; but it gave her some peaceful, painless moments when such were rare; and it left her, with everything coming back to her, it is true, but with a grateful heart. So grateful, indeed, was Gladys that she forgot to express her thanks until Miss Travers smilingly asked her how she liked that song; and then, instead of answering, she went over to where Lady Bligh was sitting, bent down, and asked a question, which was answered in a whisper.

Then Gladys came back to the piano. "Yes, I *do* like that song, very, very much; and I beg your pardon for not answering you, Miss Travers, but I was thinking of something else; and I want you, please, to sing Mendelssohn's 'Hear my Prayer!'" These words came quickly—they were newly learnt from Lady Bligh.

Miss Travers could not repress a smile. "Do you know what you are asking me for?"

"Yes; for what we heard in church last Sunday evening. That's the name, because I've just asked Lady Bligh. I would rather you sang that than anything else in the world!"

"But—" Miss Travers was puzzled by the Bride's expression; she would have given anything not to refuse, yet what could she do? "But—it isn't the sort of thing one can sit down and sing—*really* it isn't. It wants a chorus, and it is very long and elaborate."

"Yes?" Gladys seemed strangely disappointed. "But there was one part—the part I liked—where the chorus didn't come in, I am sure. It was sung by a boy. You could do it so much better! It was about the wings of a dove, and the wilderness. You know, I come from the wilderness myself"—the Bride smiled faintly—"and I thought I'd never heard anything half so lovely before; though of course I've heard very little."

"No matter how little you have heard, you will never hear anything much more beautiful than that," said Miss Travers, with sympathetic enthusiasm.

"Since I cannot hear it now, however, there is an end of it."

Gladys sighed, but her eyes pleaded still; it was impossible to look in them long and still resist. Miss Travers looked but for a moment, then, turning round to the keys, she softly touched a chord. "I will try the little bit you liked," she whispered, kindly, "whatever I make of it!"

What she did make of it is unimportant, except in its effect upon Gladys. This effect was very different from that produced a few minutes before by the song; this, at least, was no mere titillation of the senses by agreeable sounds. And it differed quite as much from the effect produced by the same thing in church on Sunday, when Gladys, after being surprised into listening, had listened only to the words. Then, indeed, the music had seemed sweet and sad, but to-night each note palpitated with a shivering, tremulous yearning, dropping into her soul a relief as deep as that of sorrow unbosomed, a comfort as soothing as the comfort of tears. And there was now an added infinity of meaning in the words; though it was the words that had thrilled her then—then, before she had brought all the present misery to pass.

> *O for the wings, for the wings of a dove!*
> *Far away, far away would I rove:*
> *In the wilderness build me a nest,*
> *And remain there for ever at rest.*

It is only a few bars, the solo here; and at the point where the chorus catches up the refrain Miss Travers softly ceased. She turned round slowly on the stool, then rose up quickly in surprise. Her ardent listener was gone. And as Miss Travers stood by the piano, peering with raised eyebrows into every corner of the room, and out into the night through the open French window, the men entered the room in a body—she was surrounded.

But Gladys had stepped softly through the window on to the lawn, re-entered the house by another way, and stolen swiftly up to her room. The last strains came to her through the open window of the drawing-room, and in at her own window, at which Gladys now knelt: and this short passage through the outer air brought them upward on the breath of the night, rarefied and softened as though from the lips of far-off angels: and so they reached her trembling ears.

The scent of roses was in the air. The moon was rising, and its rays spanned the river with a broad bridge of silver, against which some of the foliage at the garden-end stood out in fine filigree. It was a heavenly night; it was a sweet and tranquil place; but yet—

> *O for the wings of a dove!*

Gladys had been home-sick before; she had been miserable and desperate for many, many hours; but at this moment it seemed as though hitherto she had never known what it was to pant and pray in real earnest for her old life and her own country. She was almost as a weak woman in the transports of spiritual fervour, her vision riveted upon some material mental picture, the soul for one ecstatic instant separated from the flesh—only Gladys missed the ecstasy.

There was no light in the room; and the girl remained so entirely motionless, as she knelt, that her glossy head, just raised above the level of the sill, would have seemed in the moonlight a mere inanimate accessory, if it had been seen at all. But only the bats could have seen Gladys, and they did not; at all events, it was the touch of a bat's wing upon the forehead that recalled her to herself, making her aware of voices within earshot, immediately below her window. Her room was over the dining-room. The voices were men's voices, and the scent of cigars reached her as well. She could hear distinctly, but she never would have listened had she not heard her own name spoken; and then—the weakness of the moment prevented her from rising.

"No," said one of the voices, "not a bit of it; oh dear, no! Gladys has her good points; and, frankly, I am getting rather to like her. But she is impossible in her position. The whole thing was a fearful mistake, which poor old Alfred will live to repent."

The voice was unmistakable; it was Granville's.

"But"—and the other voice was that of Granville's most intimate friend, whom he had introduced to Gladys during the course of the afternoon—"doesn't he repent it already, think you?"

"Upon my word, I'm not sure that he doesn't," said Granville.

"If you ask me," said his friend, "I should say there isn't a doubt of it. I've been watching him pretty closely. Mark my words, he's a miserable man!"

"Well, I'm half inclined to agree with you," said Granville. "I didn't think so two or three days since, but now I do. You see, there are camels' backs and there are last straws (though I wish there were no proverbs); and there never was a heavier straw than yesterday's—'gad! 'twas as heavy as the rest of the load! I mean the perfectly awful scene in the Park, which you know about, and the whole town knows about, and the low papers will publish, confound them! Yes, I believe you're right; he *can't* get over this."

"Poor chap!" said Granville's friend.

"You may well say that. Alfred is no genius"—Granville was, apparently—"but he has position; he has money—luckily for him; he means to settle down in the country somewhere, and, no doubt, he'd like to be somebody in the county. But how could he? Look at his wife!"

"There ought to be a separation," said the friend, feelingly.

"Well, I don't think it's quite as bad as that," said Granville, wearing ship. "Anyway, there never will be one; you may trust her for that. And, I must own, I don't think it's all the main chance with her, either; they're sufficiently spooney. Why, she will not even leave him for a week on a visit, though, as I understand, he's doing his best to persuade her to."

Gladys's hands tightened upon the woodwork of the window-frame.

"Can't persuade her to?" cried the friend. "What did I tell you? Why, Lord love you, he wants to get rid of her already!"

This was rather strong, even for an intimate friend, and even though the intimate friend had drunk a good deal of wine. Granville's tone cooled suddenly.

"We'll drop the subject, I think. My cigar's done, and you've smoked as much as is good for you. You can do as you like, but I'm going inside."

Their footsteps sounded down the gravel-path; then the sound ceased; they had gone in by the drawing-room window.

Gladys had never once altered her position; she did not alter it now. The moon rose high in the purple sky, and touched her head with threads of silver. It was as though gray hairs had come upon her while she knelt. The sudden turning of the door-handle, and a quick step upon the threshold, aroused her. It was Alfred come for an easier coat. The people were gone.

"What—*Gladys!*" he cried. She rose stiffly to her feet, and confronted him with her back to the moonlight. "Up here—alone?"

"You didn't miss me, then?" Her tone was low and hoarse—the words ran into one another in their hurried, eager utterance.

"Why, no," cried Alfred; "to tell you the truth, I didn't."

He seemed to her in better spirits than he had been all day; his voice was full and cheery, and his manner brisk. Why? Evidently the evening had gone off very agreeably. Why? Was it because he had got rid of her for an hour? Was it, then, true that he was doing his best to get rid of her for a week—that he would be only too glad to get rid of her for ever? It was as though a poniard were being held to her breast. She paused, and nerved herself to speak calmly, before, as it were, baring her bosom to the steel.

"Alfred," she said at length, with slow distinctness, but not with the manner of one who is consciously asking a question of life or death, "I have been thinking it over, about the Barringtons; and I think I *should* like to go to them on Saturday after all. May I go?"

"May you?" Alfred fairly shouted. "I am only too delighted, Gladdie! Of course you may."

The poniard went in—to the hilt.

So delighted was Alfred that he caught her in his arms and kissed her. Her cheek was quite cold, her frame all limp. Though she reeled on her feet, she seemed to shrink instinctively from his support.

"What's the matter, Gladdie?" he cried, in sudden alarm. "What's wrong—are you ill? Stop, I'll fetch—"

She interrupted him in a whisper.

"Fetch no one." She dropped one hand upon the dressing-table, leant her weight upon it, and motioned him back with the other. "I am not ill; I only was faint, just for a moment. I am all right now. There, that's a long breath; I can speak quite properly again. You see, it was only a passing faintness. I must have fallen asleep by the window. I was enjoying the lovely night, and that must have done it. There, I am only tired now, and want—sleep!"

THAT ACID HAD BEEN APPLIED, and not in drops. Its work was complete.

XV

The First Parting

It was Saturday forenoon, and everything was ready for the departure of Gladys. Moreover, the moment had come. Garrod was at the door with the carriage; the phlegmatic stable-boy, having performed feats of unsuspected strength with the luggage, had retired into his own peculiar shell, and lurked in sullen humility at the far side of the horse; while Mr. Dix figured imposingly in the hall. Alfred was here too, waiting for Gladys to come down. But Gladys was upstairs saying good-bye to Lady Bligh, and lingering over the parting somewhat strangely, for one who was going away for a week only.

"If I hear any more such absurd talk," Lady Bligh said at last, and with some impatience, "about forgiveness and the like, I shall punish you by not allowing you to leave me at all."

"It is too late to do that," Gladys hastily put in. "But oh, Lady Bligh! if only you knew how happy you have made me—how happily I go away, having your forgiveness for everything, for everything—"

"Except for what you are saying now. How wildly you do talk, child! One would think you were going for ever."

"Who knows, Lady Bligh? There are accidents every day. That's why I'm thankful to be leaving like this."

Lady Bligh hated sentimentality. Only the intense earnestness of the girl's voice and manner restrained her from laughing; sentimentality was only fit to be laughed at; but this was sentimentality of a puzzling kind.

A minute later, with passionate kisses and incoherent expressions, out of all proportion to the occasion, and fairly bewildering to poor Lady Bligh, Gladys was gone.

Alfred scanned her narrowly as they drove to the station. By the way she kept turning round to gaze backward, you would have thought her anxious to "see the last of" things, as small boys are when the holidays are over, and bigger boys when they go finally out into the world. Alfred was going with her to Liverpool Street. She had refused to go at all if he took her (as he wanted to) all the way into Suffolk, to return himself by the next train.

"Gladdie," he said, after watching her closely, "you look cut up; is it from saying good-bye to the *mater*?"

"I suppose it must be—if I really look like that."

"There is still, perhaps, some soreness—"

"No, there is none now," said Gladys, quickly.

"Then what is it?"

"Only that it is so dreadful, saying good-bye!"

"My darling!—by the way you talk you might be going for good and all. And it is only for a week."

She did not answer, but pressed the hand that closed over her own.

During the half-hour's run to Waterloo he continued to glance furtively, and not without apprehension, at her face. It was unusually pale; dark rings encircled the eyes, and the eyes were unusually brilliant.

They had a compartment to themselves. He held her hand all the way, and she his, like a pair of moonstruck young lovers; and, for the most part, they were as silent.

"You have not been yourself these last few days," he said at length; "I am glad you are going."

"And I am glad of that," she answered.

Her tone was odd.

"But I shall be wretched while you are gone," he quickly added.

She made no reply to this; it seemed to her an afterthought. But, if it was, it grew upon him with swift and miserable effect as the minutes remaining to them gradually diminished. When they drove up to Liverpool Street he was in the depths of dejection.

It was their first parting.

She insisted on sending the necessary telegram to the Barringtons herself. His depression made him absent, and even remiss. He stood listlessly by while she filled in the form; at any other time he would have done this for her, or at least looked over her shoulder—humorously to check the spelling; but this afternoon he was less attentive in little things than she had ever known him, because she had never known him so depressed.

It was their first parting.

He had got her a compartment to herself, but only at her earnest insistence; *he* had spoken for a carriage full of people, or the one reserved for ladies—anything but solitary confinement. It was the Cambridge train; there were few stoppages and no changes.

Gladys was ensconced in her corner. For the moment, her husband sat facing her. Four minutes were left them.

"You have a Don in the next carriage to you; an ancient and wonderfully amiable one, I should say," observed Alfred, with a sickly attempt at levity. "I wish you were under his wing, my dear!"

Gladys made a respondent effort, an infinitely harder one. "No, thanks," she said; "not *me*!"

"Come, I say! Is it nervousness or vanity?"

"It is neither."

"Yet you look nervous, Gladdie, joking apart—and, honestly, I never felt less like joking in my life. And you are pale, my darling; and your hand is so cold!"

She withdrew the hand.

But one more minute was left. "Better get out, sir," said the guard, "and I'll lock the lady in."

Gladys felt a shiver pass through her entire frame. With a supreme effort she controlled herself. They kissed and clasped hands. Then Alfred stepped down heavily on to the platform.

The minute was a long one; these minutes always are. It was an age in passing, a flash to look back upon. These minutes are among the strangest accomplishments of the sorcerer Time.

"It is dreadful to let you go alone, darling, like this," he said, standing on the foot-board and leaning in. "At least you ought to have had Bunn with you. You might have given way in that, Gladdie."

"No," she whispered tremulously; "I—I like going alone."

"You must write at once, Gladdie."

"To-morrow; but you could only get it latish on Monday."

The bell was ringing. You know the clangour of a station bell; of all sounds the last that it resembles is that of the funeral knell; yet this was its echo in the heart of Gladys.

"Well, it's only for a week, after all, isn't it, Gladdie? It will be the weariest week of my life, I know. But I shan't mind—after all, it's my own doing—if only you come back with a better colour. You have been so pale, Gladdie, these last few days—pale and excitable. But it's only a week, my darling, eh?"

She could not answer.

The guard blew his whistle. There was an end of the minute at last.

"Stand back," she whispered: her voice was stifled with tears.

"Back?"—Alfred peered up into her face, and a sudden pallor spread upon his own—"with your dear eyes full of tears, where I never yet saw tears before? Back?—God forgive me for thinking of it, I'll come with you yet!"

He made as though to dive headlong through the window; but, looking him full in the eyes through her tears, his girl-wife laid a strong hand on each of his shoulders and forced him back. He staggered as the platform came under his feet. The train was already moving. He stood and gazed.

Gladys was waving to him, and smiling through her tears. So she continued until she could see him no more. Then she fell back upon the cushions, and, for a time, consciousness left her.

It was their first parting.

XVI

Traces

Alfred did not become unconscious, nor even feel faint: he was a man. But he did feel profoundly wretched. He tried to shake off this feeling, but failed. Later, on his way back through the City, he stopped somewhere to try and lunch it off, and with rather better success. He was a man: he proceeded to throw the blame upon the woman. It was Gladys who had supplied all the sentiment (and there had been an absurd amount of it) at their parting; it was the woman who had exaggerated this paltry week's separation, until it had assumed, perhaps for them both—at the moment—abnormal dimensions; he, the man, was blameless. If *his* way had obtained, she should have gone away in highest spirits, instead of in tears—and all for one insignificant week! He should write her a serious, if not a severe, letter on the subject. So Alfred went down to Twickenham in quite a valiant mood to face his week of single-blessedness, and to affect a droll appreciation of it in the popular, sprightly manner of the long-married man.

But the miserable feeling returned—if, indeed, it had ever been chased fairly away; and it returned with such force that Alfred was obliged to own at last that it, too, was exaggerated and out of all proportion to the exciting cause. He, in his turn, was sentimentalising as though Gladys had gone for a term of years. He was conscious of this; but he could not help it. His thoughts seemed bound to the parting of this Saturday, powerless to fly forward to the reunion of the next. A vague, dim sense of finality was the restraining bond; but this sense was not long to remain dim or vague. Meanwhile, so far as Alfred was concerned, the Sunday that followed was wrapped in a gloom that not even the genial presence of the distinguished (but jocular) guest could in any way pierce or dissipate. Nevertheless, it contained the last tranquil moments that Alfred was to know at that period of his life; for it led him to the verge of an ordeal such as few men are called upon to undergo.

He was not a little surprised on the Monday morning to find among the letters by the first post one addressed to his wife. She had received scarcely any letters since her arrival in England—two or three from tradesmen, an invitation or so, nothing from Australia; but this letter was directed in a large, bold hand, with which Alfred fancied he was not wholly unfamiliar; and he suddenly remembered that he had seen it before in Miss Barrington's note of invitation. Now, the post-mark bore the name of the town to which Gladys had booked from Liverpool Street, and the date of the day before; and how could Miss Barrington write to Gladys at Twickenham, when Gladys was staying with Miss Barrington in Suffolk?

He tore open the envelope, and his hand shook as he did so. When he had read to the end of the letter, which was very short, his face was gray and ghastly; his eyes were wild and staring; he sank helplessly into a chair. The note ran thus:—

Dearest Glad,

　　We are *so* disappointed, you can't think. As for me, I've been in the sulks ever since your telegram came this afternoon. What *ever can* have prevented your coming, at the *very last minute*—for your wire from *Liverpool Street*? Do write at once, for I'm *horribly* anxious, to your loving

Ada

PS.—And do *come* at once, if it's nothing serious.

Saturday

Alfred read the letter a second time, and an extraordinary composure came over him.

He folded the letter, restored it to its envelope, and put the envelope in his pocket. Then he looked at the clock. It wanted a quarter to eight. The Judge was no doubt up and about somewhere; but none of the others were down. Alfred rang the bell, and left word that he had received a letter begging an early interview on important business, and that he would breakfast in town.

Alfred was stunned; but he had formed a plan. This plan he proceeded to put into effect; or rather, once formed, the plan evolved itself into mechanical action without further thought. For some hours following he did not perfectly realise either what he was doing or why he was doing it. He never thoroughly pulled himself together, until a country conveyance, rattling him through country lanes, whisked into a wooded drive, and presently past a lawn where people were playing lawn-tennis, and so to the steps of a square, solid, country house. But he had all his wits about him, and those sharpened to the finest possible point, when he looked to see whether Gladys was, or was not, among the girls on the lawn. She was not. That was settled. He got out and rang the bell. He inquired for Mr. Barrington; Mr. Barrington was playing at lawn-tennis. In answer to a question from the butler, Bligh said that he would rather see Mr. Barrington in the house than go to him on the tennis-court. He could wait until the set was finished. He had come from London expressly to speak for a few minutes with Mr. Barrington. His name would keep until Mr. Barrington came; but he was from Australia.

The last piece of information was calculated to fetch Mr. Barrington at once; and it did. He came as he was, in his flannels, his thick hairy arms bare to the elbow: a bronzed, leonine man of fifty, with the hearty, hospitable manner of the Colonial "squatocracy." Alfred explained in a few words who he was, and why he had come. He had but one or two questions to ask, and he asked them with perfect self-possession. They elicited the assurance that nothing had been heard of Gladys in that quarter, beyond the brief message received on the Saturday. Mr. Barrington found the telegram, and handed it to his visitor. It read: "Prevented coming at last moment. Am writing—Gladys." By the time of despatch, Bligh knew that it was the message she had written out in his presence.

"Of course she never wrote?" he said coolly to the squatter.

"We have received nothing," was the grave answer.

"Yet she started," said Alfred. "I put her in the train myself, and saw her off."

His composure was incredible. The Australian was more shaken than he.

"Did you make any inquiries on the line?" asked Barrington, after a pause.

"Inquiries about what?"

"There might have been—an accident."

Bligh tapped the telegram with his finger. "This points to no accident," he said, grimly. "But," he added, more thoughtfully, "one might make inquiries down the line, as you say. It might do good to make inquiries all along the line."

"Do you mean to say you have made *none*?"

"None," said Alfred, fetching a deep sigh. "I came here straight. I could think of nothing else but getting here—and—perhaps—finding her! I thought—I thought there might be some—mistake!" His voice suddenly broke. The futility of the hope that had sustained him for hours had dawned upon him slowly, but now the cruel light hid nothing any longer. She was not here; she had not been heard of here; and precious hours had been lost. He grasped his hat and held out his trembling hand.

"Thank you! Thank you, Mr. Barrington! Now I must be off."

"Where to?"

"To Scotland Yard. I should have gone there first. But—I was mad, I think; I thought there had been some mistake. Only some mistake!"

The squatter was touched to the soul. "I have known her, off and on, since she was a baby," he said. "Bligh—if you would only let me, I should like to come with you."

Alfred wrung the other's hand, but refused his offer.

"No. Though I am grateful indeed, I would rather go alone. It would do no good, your coming; I should prefer to be alone. So only one word more. Your daughter was a great friend of Gladys; better not tell her anything of this. For it may still be only some wild freak, Mr. Barrington—God knows what it is!"

It was evening when he reached London. A whole day had been wasted. He stated his case to the police; and then there was no more to be done that night. With an eagerness that all at once became feverish he hastened back to Twickenham. It was late when he arrived at the house; only Granville was up; and, for an instant, Granville thought his brother had been drinking. The delusion lasted no longer than that instant. It was not drink with Alfred: his excitement was suppressed: he stood staring at Granville with a questioning, eager expression, as though he expected news. What could it mean? What could be the explanation of such fierce excitement in stolid Alfred, of all people in the world?

Granville thought of the one thing, or rather of the one person, likely, and threw out a feeler:—

"Have you heard from Gladys?"

"No," said Alfred, in a hollow voice. "*Have you seen her?*"

This was the last idea that had possessed him: that Gladys might have come home, that he might find her there on his return. It was the second time that day that he had cheated himself with vain, unreasoning hopes.

"Seen her?" Granville screwed in his eyeglass tighter. "Of course I haven't seen her! How should we see her here, my good fellow, when she's down in Suffolk?"

Alfred turned pale, and for an instant stood glaring; then he burst into a harsh laugh.

"You know how odd she is, Gran! I thought she might have tired of her friends and come back. She's capable of it, and I feared it—that's all!"

He left the room abruptly.

"Poor chap!" said Granville, with a sentient shake of the head; "he *is* far gone, if you like."

NEXT MORNING ALFRED WALKED INTO Scotland Yard as the clocks were striking eleven. His appointment was for that hour, and he had striven successfully to keep it to the second; though commonly he was a far from punctual man. In point of fact, he had been sitting and loitering about the Embankment for a whole hour, waiting until the moment of his appointment should come, as unwilling to go to it a minute before the time as a minute late. So he entered the Yard while Big Ben was striking. And this was a young man with a reputation for unpunctuality, and all-round unbusinesslike, dilatory habits.

Moreover, for a man who, as a rule, was not fastidious enough about such matters, his appearance this morning was wellnigh immaculate. Yet, perhaps, he had only sought, by a long and elaborate toilet, to while away the long, light hours of the early morning: for, on looking at him closely, it was impossible to believe that he had slept a wink. The fact is, abnormal circumstances had conduced to bring about in Alfred an entirely abnormal state of mind. In a word, and a trite one, he was no longer himself. A crust of insensibility had hardened upon him. Had there been no news for him at all at the Yard this morning, possibly this crust might have been broken through: for he was better prepared for one crushing blow than for the bruises of repeated disappointment. Thus, the very worst news might have affected him less, at the moment, than no news, which is supposed, popularly, to be of the best. But there was some news.

Official investigation had thus far discovered what a person of average intelligence, with a little more presence of mind than Alfred had shown, might have ascertained, perhaps for himself. Yet the information was important. Gladys had left the train, with her luggage, two stations before her destination. This was testified by the guard of the train. But there was a later fact still. It was certain that Gladys had returned to town by the next up-train: for she had personally deposited her luggage in the cloak-room at Liverpool Street between the hours of six and seven on the Saturday evening. There all trace of her was lost, for the present; but it was extremely likely that fresh traces would be forthcoming during the course of the day.

The simple nature of the inquiries that had elicited the above information will be at once apparent; but Alfred went away with an exalted opinion of the blood-hound sagacity of the police. In his present condition of mind, his opinion, good or bad, was not worth much. He went to a club which he had not been in for years, and of which he had long ceased to look upon himself as a member; but his bankers, doubtless, still paid his subscription; and in any case it was not likely that he would be turned out. He would find some quiet corner and sit down and wait until the messenger came from Scotland Yard; for, of course, something more would be discovered during the course of the day—had they not promised as much? The quiet corner that he chose was an upstairs window, from which there was a fair glimpse of the river. The river fascinated him most strangely to-day. During the hour he had loitered on the Embankment, between ten and eleven, he had raised his eyes but seldom from the river.

He sat long at the window—so long that minutes ran into hours and the summer afternoon melted into the summer evening. The room was a reading-room; the windows were in snug recesses. Alfred had his recess to himself for hours and hours. He was conscious of no other presence; certainly no one spoke to him: very possibly, with his beard, no one recognised him.

The sun was sinking. He could not see it from this window; but he could see the heightened contrast of light and shadow among the ripples of the river, and the shadows deepening far away under Westminster Bridge. This was where his gaze rested. It was a stony gaze; his lips were compressed and bloodless, his features pointed and pale. A hideous vision filled his mind; but it was a vision only; it had no meaning. He did not realise it. He realised nothing. . . Some one came and asked if he was Mr. Bligh. It was a club servant. A man awaited him below. Alfred went down; the messenger from Scotland Yard was come at last.

The messenger was the bearer of these few words:—

"A lady's hat and jacket have been found in the river below Blackwall. If you wish to see them, they are here."

Five minutes later Alfred walked into the office in which he had heard the result of the investigations that morning, and identified instantly the jacket and hat awaiting his inspection.

Gladys had gone away in them on Saturday.

XVII

Waiting for the Worst

For the second time, it was Granville whom Alfred first encountered on his return from town. They met in the twilight. Dinner was over, and Granville sauntered alone in the bit of garden between the house and the road, smoking a cigarette. Suddenly the gate was opened, and the one brother, looking up, saw the other coming quickly towards him through the dusk.

It was too dark for the ready reading of faces; but it struck Granville that the approaching footsteps were hasty and unusual. He recalled Alfred's unaccountable manner of the night before. Indeed, all his movements, during the past two days, were mysterious: up to London first thing in the morning, back late, and not a word to any one; whereas the whole household, as a general rule, were in possession of most of Alfred's private plans and hopes and fears. But Granville had no time to speculate now. Alfred came straight up to him.

"I want to speak to you, Gran," he said. "I'm glad I found you here."

The step had been suspicious; the voice was worse. It was calm enough, but it was not Alfred's voice at all. Something had happened. Granville put up his eyeglass; but in that light it did not avail him much.

"Let us sit down, then," said Granville, leading the way to a seat under the trees.

"What is it about?"

Then Alfred began, in set tones and orderly phrases. The affectation of his manner was almost grotesque.

"I want a kind of professional opinion from you, Gran, about—let us say, about a case that interests me, rather. That will be near enough to the mark, I think."

"Delighted to help you, if I can." Granville lounged back carelessly on the garden-seat, but his keen glance lost not a line of the other's profile, as Alfred bent forward with his eyes upon the ground; and those lines seemed strangely hardened.

"Thank you. The case is, briefly, this," Alfred continued: "somebody— no matter who—has been missing for some days. The number of days is of no consequence either. The police were not informed immediately. They only heard of it last night. But, this afternoon, they found—"

Alfred checked himself, sat upright, shifted his position, and met Granville's gaze.

"What should you consider incontestable evidence of drowning, Gran?"

"The body."

"Of course. But you have to look for bodies. What should you find, to make you search with the absolute certainty of discovering the body at last?"

"Nothing else could make it an absolute certainty. But lots of things would set you searching—a hat, for instance."

"They have found her hat!" said Alfred, through his clenched teeth.

"*Her* hat! Whose?"

Alfred stretched over, caught Granville's arm in a nervous grip, and whispered rapidly in his ear. In a moment Granville knew all. But he did not speak immediately. When he did speak, it was to ask questions. And there was another unnatural voice now, besides Alfred's— Granville's was quite soft.

"Was she unhappy at all?" he asked.

"Just the reverse, I thought, until last week. You know what happened in the Park yesterday week. She said some very wild things after that, and spoke as though she had never been quite happy here; she vowed she would never forgive herself for what she had done; and she said she wished she was dead. Well, I did not think much about her words; I thought more of what she had done; I put down what she said to the shame and temper of the moment, not to real unhappiness. But, when I said good-bye to her, then she *was* unhappy—more so than I ever knew her before."

From his tone, no one could have guessed that he was speaking of his wife.

"And you think she—she—"

Granville could not bring his lips to utter the words.

Alfred could. "I think she has drowned herself," he said calmly.

Granville shuddered. Callous as he was himself by nature, callousness such as this he could not have imagined possible; it was horrible to see and to hear.

Neither spoke for some little time.

"Did it never occur to you," said Granville, at last, "that she might have drowned herself without all this trouble, simply by walking to the bottom of the garden here?"

"What?" cried Alfred, sharply. His fingers tightened upon Granville's arm. His voice fell, oddly enough, into a natural tone.

Granville repeated his question.

"No," said Alfred, hoarsely, "that never crossed my mind. But there's something in it. God bless you, Gran, for putting it into my head! It's almost like a ray of hope—the first. If I hadn't seen the things and identified them as hers—"

"The things! You did not say there was anything else besides the hat. What else was there?"

"The jacket she went away in."

"You are sure it was hers?"

"Yes."

"You could swear to both hat and jacket?"

"Yes."

Granville leapt to his feet.

"Who throw their things into the water"—he asked, in strange excitement, for him—"the people who mean to sink or the people who mean to swim—or the people who mean to stay on the bank?"

Alfred stared at him blankly. Gradually the light dawned upon him that had entered Granville's quicker intelligence in a flash.

"What do you mean?" whispered Alfred; and, in a moment, his voice and his limbs were trembling.

"Nothing very obscure," replied Granville, with a touch of contempt, which, even then, he could not manage to conceal (Alfred's slow perception always had irritated him); "simply this: Gladys has *not* drowned herself. She was never the girl to do it. She had too much sense and vitality and courage. But she may mean us to think there's an end of her—God knows with what intention. She may have gone off somewhere—God knows where. We must find out—"

He stopped abruptly, and nearly swore: for Alfred was wringing his hand, and weeping like a child.

Granville hated this, but bore it stoically. It was now plain to him that Alfred had been driven very nearly out of his senses: and no wonder—Granville himself could as yet scarcely realise or believe what he had heard. And this outburst was the natural reaction following upon an unnatural mental condition. But *was* there any ground for hope? Granville was less confident than he appeared when he amended his last words and said:—

"I *will* find out."

Alfred wrung his hand again. He was calmer now, but terribly shaken and shattered. The weakness that he had been storing up during the past two days had come over him, as it were, in the lump. Granville led him to his room. Alfred had never in his life before known Granville half so good-natured and sympathetic; he blessed him fervently.

"You were her friend," he said, huskily. "She thought no end of you, Gran! You got on so splendidly together, after the first few days; and she was always talking about you. Find her—find her for me, Gran; and God bless you—and forgive her for this trick she has played us!"

Granville did not often feel contrition, or remorse, or shame: but he felt all three just then. He knew rather too well the measure of his own kindness to Gladys. For the first time in his life—and not, perhaps, before it was time—he disliked himself heartily. He felt vaguely that, whatever had happened, he had had something to do with it. He had had more to do with it than he guessed. "I'll do my best—I'll do my best," he promised; and he meant his "best" to be better than that of the smartest detective at Scotland Yard.

He left Alfred, shut himself up alone, and reviewed the situation. An hour's hard thinking led to a rather ingenious interview—one with the girl Bunn. It took place on the stairs, of all places. Granville saw her set foot upon the bottom stair; he immediately sat down upon the top one, produced a newspaper, and blocked the gangway.

"Bunn, you have a sweetheart in Australia. Don't pout and toss your head; it's nothing to be ashamed of—quite the contrary; and it's the fact, I think—eh?"

"Lor', Mr. Granville, what if I have?"

"Well, nothing; only there is something about it in this newspaper— about Australia, I mean; not about you—that's to come. You shall have the newspaper, Bunn; here it is. I thought you'd like it, that's all."

Bunn took the paper, all smiles and blushes.

"Oh, thank you, Mr. Granville. And—and I beg your pardon, sir."

"Don't name it, my good girl. But, look here, Bunn; stay one moment, if you don't mind." (She could scarcely help staying, he gave her no chance of passing; besides, he had put her under an obligation.) "Tell me now, Bunn—didn't Mrs. Alfred know something about him? And didn't Mrs. Alfred talk to you a good deal about Australia?"

"That she did, sir. But she didn't know my young man, Mr. Granville. She only got his address from me just as she was going away, sir."

"Ah! she wanted his address before she went away, did she?"

"Yes, sir. She said she would name him in writing to her father, or in speaking to Mr. Barrington, or that, any way, it'd be nice to have it, against ever she went out there again, sir."

"Oh, she gave three reasons all in one, eh? And did she say she'd like to go out again, Bunn?"

"She always said that, sir, between ourselves—'between you and I, Bella,' it used to be. But, time I gave her the address, she went on as if she would like to go, and meant a-going, the very next day."

"Yet she didn't like leaving this, even for a week—eh, Bunn?"

"Lor', no, sir! She spoke as if she was never coming back no more. And she kissed me, Mr. Granville—she did, indeed, sir; though I never named that in the servants' hall. She said there might be a accident, or somethink, and me never see her no more; but that, if ever she went back to Australia, she'd remember my young man, and get him a good billet. Them were her very words. But, oh, Mr. Granville!—oh, sir!—"

"There, there. Don't turn on the waterworks, Bunn. I thought Mrs. Alfred had been cut up about something; but I wasn't sure—that's why I asked *you*, Bunn; though I think, perhaps, you needn't name this conversation either in the servants' hall, or tell any one else what you have told me. Yes, you may go past now. But—stop a minute, Bunn—here's something else that you needn't name in the servants' hall."

The something else was a half-sovereign.

"It was worth it, too," said Granville, when the girl was gone; "she has given me something to go upon. These half-educated and impulsive people always do let out more to their maids than to any one else."

He went back to Alfred.

"There was something I forgot to ask you. How much money do you suppose Gladys had about her when she went away?"

"I have no idea," said Alfred.

"Do you know how much money you have given her since you have been over—roughly?"

"No; I don't know at all."

"Think, man. Fifty pounds?"

"I should say so. I gave her a note or so whenever it struck me she might want it. She never would ask."

"Do you think she spent much?"

"I really can't tell you, Gran; perhaps not a great deal, considering everything; for, when I was with her, I never would let her shell out. I never knew of her spending much; but she had it by her, in case she wanted it; and that was all I cared about."

And that was all Granville cared about. He ceased his questioning; but he was less ready to leave Alfred alone than he had been before. He had found him sitting in the dark by the open window, and staring blankly into the night. Granville had insisted on lighting the gas: only to see how the room was filled with Gladys's things. In every corner of it some woman's trifle breathed of her. Granville felt instinctively that much of this room, in the present suspense, might turn a better brain than Alfred's, in Alfred's position.

"Look here," said Granville, at last: "I have been thinking. Listen, Alfred."

"Well?" said Alfred absently, still gazing out of window.

"I have got a theory," went on Granville—"no matter what; only it has nothing to say to death or drowning. It is a hopeful theory. I intend to practise it at once: in a day or two it ought to lead me to absolute certainty of one thing, one way or the other. No matter what that one thing is; I have told you what it is not. Now, I shall have to follow out my idea in town; and if I find the truth at all, I shall most likely come across it suddenly, round a corner as it were. So I have been thinking that you may as well be in town too, to be near at hand in case I am successful. If you still have a club, you might hang about there, and talk to men, and read the papers; if not—Why do you shake your head?"

"I am not going to town any more," said Alfred, in low, decided tones. "If you are right, and she is not dead, she may come back—she may come back! Then I shall be here to meet her—and—and—But you understand me, Gran?"

"Not very well," said Granville, dryly, and with a shrug of his shoulders that was meant to shift from them all responsibility for Alfred's possible insanity. "In your case I should prefer to be in town rather than here. However, a man judges for himself. There is one thing, however; if you stay here all day—"

"What's that?"

"The question whether you should tell the Judge and the *mater*."

"No," said Alfred, resolutely; "I shall not tell them—not, that is, until the worst is known for certain. They think she is at the Barringtons'. I shall say I have heard from her. I would tell a million lies to save them the tortures of uncertainty that I am suffering, and shall suffer, till—till we know the worst. Oh, Granville!—for God's sake, find it out quickly!"

"I'll do my best—I've already told you I would," said Granville almost savagely; and he left the room.

Granville's best, in matters that required a clear head and some little imagination, was always excellent. In the present instance his normal energies were pushed to abnormal lengths by the uncomfortable feeling that he himself had been not unconcerned in bringing about that state of unhappiness which alone could have driven his sister-in-law to her last rash, mysterious step; by a feverish desire to atone, if the smallest atonement were possible; and by other considerations, which, for once, were unconnected with the first person singular. Nevertheless, on the Wednesday—the day following the foregoing conversation—he found out nothing at all; and nothing at all on the Thursday. Then Alfred made up his mind that nothing but the very worst could now come to light, and that that was only a question of time; and he fell into an apathy, by day, that Granville's most vigorous encouragement, in the evening, could do nothing to correct. Thus, when the news did come, when the terrible suspense was suddenly snapped, Alfred was, perhaps, as ill-prepared for a shock (though he had expected one for days) as it was possible for a man to be.

It was on the Friday night. Lady Bligh and Sir James were deep in their game of *bezique*. Alfred sat apart from them, without a hope left in his heart, and marvellously altered in the face. His pallor was terrible, but perhaps natural; but already his cheekbones, which were high, seemed strangely prominent; and the misery in his large still eyes cried out as it sometimes does from the eyes of dumb animals in pain. He was conscious of his altered looks, perhaps; for he sedulously avoided looking his parents in the face. They did not know yet. It added to his own anguish to think of the anguish that must come to them too, sooner or later—sooner now—very soon indeed.

The door opened. Granville entered, with a brisk, startling step, and a face lit up—though it was Granville's face—with news.

Alfred saw him—saw his face—and rose unsteadily to his feet.

"Speak! Say you have found her! No—I see it in your face—she is there. Let me come to her!"

As Alfred stepped forward, Granville recoiled, and the light left his face.

Alfred turned to his parents. The Judge had risen, and glanced in mute amazement from one son to the other: both were pale, but their looks told nothing. Lady Bligh sat back in her chair, her smooth face wrinkled with bewilderment and vague terror.

"It is Gladys come back," said Alfred, in tremulous explanation; "it is only that Gladys has come back, mother!"

Even then he chuckled in his sleeve to think that they had never known, and never need know, anything of this, the worst of his wife's many and wild escapades.

But Granville recoiled still farther, and his face became gray.

"I have not seen her," he said, solemnly. "She is *not* here."

"Not seen her? Not here?" Alfred was quickly sobered. "But you know where she is? I see it in your face. She is within reach—eh? Come, take me to her!"

"She is not even within reach," Granville answered, squeezing out the words by a strenuous effort. "I cannot take you to her. Gladys sailed for Australia last Monday morning!"

Alfred sunk heavily into a chair. No one spoke. No one was capable of speech. Before any one had time to think, Alfred was on his feet again, tottering towards the door.

"I must follow!" he whispered, in hoarse, broken tones. "I will follow her to-night! Stand aside, Gran; thanks; and God bless you! Good-bye! I shall know where to find her out there. I have no time to stop!"

Granville stood aside in obedience; but for one instant only: the next—he sprang forward to catch in his arms the falling form of Alfred.

XVIII

The Boundary-Rider of the Yelkin Paddock

Picture the Great Sahara. The popular impression will do: it has the merit of simplicity: glaring desert, dark-blue sky, vertical sun, and there you are. Omit the mirage and the thirsty man; but, instead, mix sombre colours and work up the African desert into a fairly desirable piece of Australian sheep-country.

This, too, is a simple matter. You have only to cover the desert with pale-green saliferous bushes, no higher than a man's knee; quite a scanty covering will do, so that in the thickest places plenty of sand may still be seen; and there should be barren patches to represent the low sand-hills and the smooth clay-pans. Then have a line of low-sized dark-green scrub at the horizon; but bite in one gleaming, steely speck upon this sombre rim.

Conceive this modification of the desert, and you have a fair notion of the tract of country—six miles by five—which was known on Bindarra Station as the "Yelkin Paddock," the largest paddock in the "C Block."

Multiply this area by six; divide and subdivide the product by wire fences, such as those that enclose the Yelkin Paddock; water by means of excavations and wells and whims; stock with the pure merino and devastate with the accursed rabbit; and (without troubling about the homestead, which is some miles north of the Yelkin) you will have as good an idea of the Bindarra "run," as a whole, as of its sixth part, the paddock under notice.

The conspicuous mark upon the distant belt of dingy low-sized forest—the object that glitters in the strong sunlight, so that it can be seen across miles and miles of plain—is merely the galvanised-iron roof of a log-hut, the hut that has been the lodging of the boundary-rider of the Yelkin Paddock ever since the Yelkin Paddock was fenced.

A boundary-rider is not a "boss" in the Bush, but he is an important personage, in his way. He sees that the sheep in his paddock "draw" to the water, that there is water for them to draw to, and that the fences and gates are in order. He is paid fairly, and has a fine, free, solitary life. But no boundary-rider had ever stopped long at the Yelkin hut. The solitude was too intense. After a trial of a few weeks—sometimes days—the man invariably rolled up his blankets, walked in to the homestead, said that there was moderation in all things, even in solitude, and demanded his cheque. The longest recorded term of office in the Yelkin Paddock was six months; but that boundary-rider had his reasons: he was wanted by the police. When, after being captured in the hut, this man was tried and hanged for a peculiarly cold-blooded murder, the Yelkin post became even harder to fill than it had been before.

During the Australian summer following that other summer which witnessed the events of the previous chapters, this post was not only filled for many months by the same boundary-rider, but it was better filled than it had ever been before. Moreover, the boundary-rider was thoroughly satisfied, and even anxious to remain. The complete solitude had been far less appreciated by the gentleman with the rope round his neck; for him it had terrors. The present boundary-rider knew no terrors. The solitude was more than acceptable; the Crusoe-like existence was entirely congenial; the level breezy plains, the monotonous procession of brilliant, blazing days, and the life of the saddle and the hut, were little less than delightful, to the new boundary-rider in the Yelkin. They were the few pleasures left in a spoilt life.

There could have been no better cabin for "a life awry" (not even in the Bush, the living sepulchre of so many such) than the Yelkin hut. But it was not the place to forget in. There are, however, strong natures that can never forget, and still live on. There are still stronger natures that do not seek to forget, yet retain some of the joy of living side by side with the full sorrow of remembrance. The boundary-rider's was one of these.

The boundary-rider saw but few faces from the home-station; none from anywhere else. But, one glowing, hot-wind day, early in January, a mounted traveller entered the Yelkin Paddock by the gate in the south fence. He was following the main track to the homestead, and this track crossed a corner of the Yelkin Paddock, the corner most remote from the hut. He did not seem a stranger, for he glanced but carelessly at the diverging yet conterminous wheel-marks which are the puzzling feature of all Bush roads. He was a pallid, gaunt, black-bearded man: so gaunt and so pallid, indeed, that no one would have taken him at the first glance, or at the second either, for Alfred Bligh.

Yet it was Alfred—straight, virtually, from his sick-bed. As soon as he could stand (which was not for weeks) he had been taken on board the steamer. The voyage, it was hoped, would do him good, and he was bent on going—to find his wife. It did not do him much good; the eyes that swept at last the territory of his father-in-law were the sunken, wistful eyes of a shattered man.

Nothing had been heard of Gladys. Granville, indeed, had written to Bindarra, but there had been no reply. Of this Alfred had not been informed. From the first moments of returning consciousness he had expressed himself strongly against writing at all.

So, as he crossed the corner of the Yelkin Paddock, all he knew was that Gladys had sailed for Australia six months before.

"If she is here, she is here," he muttered a hundred times; "and there will have been no warning of my coming to frighten her away. If she is not here—if she were dead—"

His eyes dropped upon the bony hand holding the reins.

"Well, it would be an easier matter to follow her there than here. It would take less time!"

But, as often as this contingency presented itself, his thin hand involuntarily tightened the reins. Indeed, the nearer he got to the homestead the slower he rode. Many a thousand times he had ridden in fancy this last stage of his long, long journey, and always at a hand-gallop; but, now that he was riding it in fact, he had not the courage to press on. He let his tired horse make the speed, and even that snail's pace was, at moments, too quick for him.

At the hour wherein he needed his utmost nerve to meet his fate—his nerve, and the stout heart that had brought him, weak as he was, from the opposite end of the earth, were failing him.

The gate in the west fence was in sight, when Alfred, awaking from a fit of absence, became aware that a man with a cylinder of rolled blankets upon his back (his "swag") was tramping along the track to meet him. For a moment Alfred's heart thumped; he would know his fate now; this man, who was evidently from the home-station, would tell him. Then he recognised the man. It was Daft Larry, the witless stockman, who, being also stone deaf, was incapable of answering questions.

Larry was a short man, strongly built though elderly, and probably less old than he looked. He had a fresh complexion, a short gray beard, and eyes as blue (and as expressionless) as the flawless southern sky. He recognised Alfred, stood in his path, threw down his swag, put his hands in his pockets, and smiled delightedly; not in surprise; in mere idiotic delight. On beholding Alfred, this had been his invariable behaviour. They had beheld one another last a year ago; but last year and yesterday were much the same date to Larry.

"I like a man that is well-bred!" exclaimed Larry, with a seraphic smile, his head critically on one side. On beholding Alfred, this had been his invariable formula.

Alfred stopped his horse.

Daft Larry cocked his head on the other side. "You're not one of the low sort!" he went on.

Alfred smiled.

"*You're* well-bred," continued Larry, in the tone of a connoisseur. Then, wagging his head gravely: "I like a man that's not one of the low sort; I like a man that is well-bred!"

That was the end, as it always had been. Larry picked up his swag with the air of a man who has proved his case.

Alfred had ridden on some yards, when a call from the idiot made him stop.

"Look there!" shouted Larry, with an ungainly sweep of the arm. "Dust-storm coming up—bad dust-storm. Don't get catched, mister—you aren't one of the low sort—not you!"

Daft Larry had been known to give gratuitous information before, though he could not answer questions. Alfred, instead of riding on, now looked about him. There was sense enough in the warning; though Larry, apparently, did not mind being "catched" himself, since he was plodding steadily on, leaving the station, probably for good, as he periodically did leave it. There was every indication of a dust-storm, though the sun still shone brilliantly. The hot-wind had become wild and rampant. It was whipping up the sandy coating of the plain in every direction. High in the air were seen whirling spires and cones of sand—a curious effect against the deep-blue sky. Below, puffs of sand were breaking out of the plain in every direction, as though the plain were alive with invisible horsemen. These sandy cloudlets were instantly dissipated by the wind; it was the larger clouds that were lifted whole into the air, and the larger clouds of sand were becoming more and more the rule.

Alfred's eye, quickly scanning the horizon, descried the roof of the boundary-rider's hut still gleaming in the sunlight. He remembered the hut well. It could not be farther than four miles, if as much as that, from this point of the track; but it was twelve miles at least from this to

E.W. HORNUNG

the homestead. He also knew these dust-storms of old; Bindarra was notorious for them. Without thinking twice, Alfred put spurs to his horse and headed for the hut. Before he had ridden half the distance, the detached clouds of sand banded together in one dense whirlwind; and it was only owing to his horse's instinct that he did not ride wide of the hut altogether; for, during the last half mile, he never saw the hut until its outline loomed suddenly over his horse's ears; and by then the sun was invisible.

"I never saw one come on quicker!" gasped Alfred, as he jumped off and tethered his quivering horse in the lee of the hut.

The excitement, and the gallop, had made Alfred's blood tingle in his veins. It was a novel sensation. He stepped briskly into the hut.

Almost his first sight on entering was the reflection of his own face in a little mirror, which was neatly nailed to the wall, close to the door. Alfred had never been vain, but he did pause to gaze at himself then; for his face was covered with a thin veneer of sand, as a wall becomes coated with driven snow. He dashed off the sand, and smiled; and for the moment, with some colour in his cheeks and a healthy light in his eyes, Alfred scarcely knew himself. Then he turned his back upon the glass, merely noting that it was a queer thing to find in a boundary-rider's hut, and that it had not been there a year ago.

The door had been ajar, and the window was blocked up. The sand, however, had found free entry through the crevices between the ill-fitting pine-logs of the walls, and already the yellow coating lay an eighth of an inch thick all over the boarded floor and upon the rude bench and table.

Alfred sat down and watched the whirling sand outside slowly deepen in tint. He had left the door open, because otherwise the interior of the hut would have been in complete darkness. As it was, it was difficult to distinguish objects; but Alfred, glancing round, was struck with the scrupulous tidiness of everything.

"Ration-bags all hung up; nothing left about; fireplace cleaned out—daily, I should say; pannikins bright as silver; bunk made up. All this is most irregular!" exclaimed Alfred. "This boundary-rider must be a curiosity. I never saw anything half so neat during all the months I was in the Bush before. One might almost suspect a woman's hand in it—especially in that mirror. Which reminds me, Gladys told me she was once out here for a week, alone, riding the boundaries, when they were short-handed. My darling! What nerve! Would to Heaven you had had less nerve!"

The thick sand rattled in continuous assault upon the iron roof. It was becoming a difficult matter to see across the hut. But the storm, and the gallop, had had a curiously exhilarating effect upon Alfred. His spirits had risen.

"I wish that boundary-rider would come in; but the storm's bound to fetch him. I want a pannikin of tea badly, to lay the dust inside; there's as much there as there was outside, I'll be bound. Besides, he will have news for me. Poor Larry!—the same old drivel! And to think that I was something like that in my delirium—that I might have been left like Larry!"

His attention was here attracted by the illustrated prints pasted upon a strip of sackcloth nailed to the pine-logs over the bunk: a feature, this, of every bushman's hut. He went over to look at them, and, the better to do so, leant with one knee upon the bed—the rudely-framed bed that was so wonderfully well "made."

"Ah!" remarked Alfred, "some of them are the old lot; I remember them. But some are new, and—why, that's a cabinet photograph down there by the pillow; and"—bending down to examine it—"good Heavens! it's of *me*!"

It was a fact. The photograph, fixed so close to the pillow, was an extremely life-like one of Alfred Bligh. But how had it got there? Of what interest or value could it be to the boundary-rider of the Yelkin Paddock? It had been taken last summer, at Richmond; and—oh, yes, he remembered now—Gladys had sent one out to her father. That was it, of course. The boundary-man had found it lying about the veranda or the yard at the homestead (Alfred knew his father-in-law), and had rescued it for the wall of his hut. No matter (to the boundary-man) who it was, it was a picture, and one that would rather set off the strip of sackcloth. That was it, of course; a simple explanation.

Yet Alfred trembled. The photograph was in a far from conspicuous position; nor did it look as if it had been left lying about. What if it belonged to Gladys? What if Gladys had fastened it there with her own hands? What if she came sometimes to the hut—this hut in which he stood? What if she had spent another week here riding the boundaries, when her father was short of men?

All at once he felt very near to her; and the feeling made him dizzy. His eyes roved once again round the place, noting the abnormal neatness and order that had struck him at first; a look of wild inquiry came into his haggard face; and even then, as the agony of surmise tightened every nerve—a sound broke plainly upon his ears. It was heard above the tinkle of the sand upon the roof: a horse's canter, muffled in the heavy sand outside.

Alfred sprang to the door. At the same instant a rider drew rein in front of him. They were not five paces apart, but such was the density of the flying sand and dust that he could see no more than the faint outline of the horse and its rider. Then the rider leapt lightly to the ground. It was the boundary-rider of the Yelkin Paddock; but the boundary-rider was a woman.

Alfred reeled forward, and clasped her to his heart.

"Gladdie! Darling!"

He had found her.

XIX

ANOTHER LETTER FROM ALFRED

Bindarra Station, N.S.W., *April 13*

Dearest Mother,

"Your dear letter, in answer to my first, written in January, has just reached me. Though I wrote so fully last mail, I can't let a mail go without some sort of an answer. But, as a matter of fact, I am in a regular old hurry. The mail-boy is waiting impatiently in the veranda, with his horse 'hung up' to one of the posts; and the store keeper is waiting in the store to drop my letter in the bag and seal it up. So I must be short. Even with lots of time, however, you know I never could write stylish, graphic letters like Gran can. So you must make double allowances for me.

"And now, dear mother, about our coming back to England; and what you propose; and what you say about my darling. To take the best first—God bless you for your loving words! I can say nothing else. Yes, I knew you were getting to love her in spite of all her waywardness; and I know—I *know*—that you would love her still. And you would love her none the less for all that has happened; you would remember what I explained in my first letter, that it was *for my sake*; you would think no longer of what she did, but why she did it.

"But, about coming back, we have, as you already know, made up our minds to live out our lives here in Australia. After all, it's a far better country—a bigger and a better Britain. There is no poverty here, or very little; you never get stuck up for coppers in the streets of the towns; or, if you do, it's generally by a newly-landed immigrant who hasn't had time to get out of bad old habits. There's more room for everybody than at home, and fairer rations of cakes and ale all round. Then there's very little ill-health, because the climate is simply perfect—which reminds me that *I* am *quite* well now—have put on nearly two stone since I landed! But all this about Australia's beside the mark: the real point is that it suits Gladdie and me better than any other country in the world.

"Now for some news. We have decided upon our station at last. It is the one in Victoria, in the north-eastern district—I think I mentioned it among the 'probables' in my last. It is not large as stations go; but 'down in Vic' you can carry as many sheep to the acre as acres to the sheep up here in the 'back-blocks.' You see, it is a grass country. But the scenery is splendid: great rugged ranges covered with the typical gum-trees, of which there are none up here, and a fine creek clean through the middle of the 'run.' Then there are parrots and 'possums and native bears all over the place, none of which you get up here, though I fear there will be more snakes too. The only drawback is the 'cockatoos.' I don't mean the *bird*, dear mother, but the 'cockatoo selectors.' Personally, I don't think these gentry are the vermin my father-in-law makes them out to be; *he* brackets them with the rabbits; but *I* mean to make friends with them—if I can. The homestead is delightful: good rooms, and broad veranda round three sides. We are going to be absurdly happy there.

"We shall not take possession though till after shearing—*i.e.* in your autumn, though the agreement is signed and everything arranged. Meanwhile, we shall stay on here, and I am to get a little more Colonial experience. I need it badly, but not perhaps so badly as my father-in-law makes out. He ridiculed the idea of my turning squatter on my own account, unless Gladys was 'boss.' But, now that we have fixed on the Victorian station, he is a bit more encouraging. He says any fool could make *that* country pay, referring of course to the rainfall, which just there, in the ranges, is one of the best in Australia. Still, he is right: experience *is* everything in the Colonies.

"So I am not quite idle. All day I am riding or driving about the 'run,' seeing after things, and keeping my eyes open. In the evenings Gladdie and I have taken to reading together. This was her doing, not mine, mind; though I won't yield to her in my liking of it. The worst of it is, it's so difficult to know where to begin; *I* am so painfully ignorant. Can *you* not help us, dear mother, with some hints? Do!—and when we come home some day (just for a trip) you will find us both such reformed and enlightened members of society!

"But, long before that, *you* must come out and see *us*. Don't shake your head. *You simply must.* England and Australia are getting nearer and nearer every year. The world's wearing small, like one of those round balls of soap, between the hands of Time—(a gem in the rough this, for Gran to polish and set!) Why, there's a Queensland squatter who for years has gone 'home' for the hunting season; while, on the other hand, Australia is becoming *the* crack place to winter in.

"Now, as you, dear mother, always *do* winter abroad, why not here as well as anywhere else? You must! You shall! If not next winter, then the following one; and if the Judge cannot bring you, then Gran must. That reminds me: how are they both? And has Gran been writing anything specially trenchant lately? I'm afraid I don't appreciate very 'cutely—'miss half the "touches,"' he used to tell me (though I think I have made him a present of a 'touch' to-day). But you know how glad we would both be to read some of his things; so *you* might send one sometimes, dear mother, without him knowing. For we owe him so much! And, besides what he did for me afterwards, he was always so nice and brotherly with Gladys. I know she thought so at the time, though she doesn't speak about him much now—I can't think why. *You're* the one she thinks of most, dearest mother; you're her model and her pattern for life!

"The mail-boy has begun to remonstrate. He'll have to gallop the whole way to the 'jolly' township, he says, if I am not quick. So I must break off; but I will answer your dear letter more fully next mail, or, better still, Gladdie shall write herself. Till then, good-bye, and dearest love from us both.

Ever your affectionate son,
Alfred

"PS.—Gladys has read the above: so one last word on the sly.

"Oh, mother, if you only saw her at this moment! She is sitting in the veranda—I can just see her through the door. She's in one of those long deck-chairs, with a book, though she seems to have tired of reading. I can't see much of her face, but only the sweep of her cheek, and the lashes of one lid, and her little ear. But I can see she isn't reading—she's threading her way through the pines into space somewhere—perhaps back to Twickenham, who knows? And she's wearing a white dress; you would like it—it's plain. And her cheek is quite brown; you'll remember how it was the day she landed from the launch. But there! I can't describe like Gran, so it's no good trying. Only I do know this: I simply love her more and more and more, and a million times more for all that has happened. And you, and all of you, and all your friends, would fairly worship her now. You couldn't help it!"

A Note About the Author

Ernest William Hornung (1866–1921) was an English author and poet, best known as a crime writer who often published under his initials, E.W. Hornung. When he was seventeen, Hornung moved to Australia, with the hope that the climate would remedy his poor health. Hornung often referred to this time as one of the best periods of his life, and he based much of his work off an Australian setting. A little over two years later, Hornung returned to England and worked as a journalist during the active period of the infamous serial killer Jack the Ripper, which likely sparked his interest in crime fiction. Hornung married Connie Doyle, the sister of major author Arthur Conan Doyle, in 1893. While the author explored many important themes in his work, the topics of Australia, crime, and cricket were commonly present in his work, signifying Hornung's interest and passion for each.

A Note from the Publisher

Spanning many genres, from non-fiction essays to literature classics to children's books and lyric poetry, Mint Edition books showcase the master works of our time in a modern new package. The text is freshly typeset, is clean and easy to read, and features a new note about the author in each volume. Many books also include exclusive new introductory material. Every book boasts a striking new cover, which makes it as appropriate for collecting as it is for gift giving. Mint Edition books are only printed when a reader orders them, so natural resources are not wasted. We're proud that our books are never manufactured in excess and exist only in the exact quantity they need to be read and enjoyed.

Discover more of your favorite classics with Bookfinity™.

- Track your reading with custom book lists.
- Get great book recommendations for your personalized Reader Type.
- Add reviews for your favorite books.
- AND MUCH MORE!

Visit **bookfinity.com** and take the fun Reader Type quiz to get started.

Enjoy our classic and modern companion pairings!

Classic & Modern